Linus and Etta Could Use a Win

Also by Caroline Huntoon
SKATING ON MARS

Linus and Etta Could Use a Win

CAROLINE HUNTOON

Feiwel and Friends
New York

A Feiwel and Friends Book
An imprint of Macmillan Publishing Group, LLC
120 Broadway, New York, NY 10271 • mackids.com

Our books may be purchased in bulk for promotional, educational,
or business use. Please contact your local bookseller or the Macmillan
Corporate and Premium Sales Department at (800) 221–7945 ext. 5442 or
by email at MacmillanSpecialMarkets@macmillan.com.

Library of Congress Cataloging-in-Publication Data

Names: Huntoon, Caroline, author.
Title: Linus and Etta could use a win / Caroline Huntoon.
Description: First edition. | New York : Feiwel & Friends, 2024. |
    Audience: Ages 8–12. | Audience: Grades 7–9. | Summary: "A hot-headed
    cynic befriends the new kid—a shy trans boy—when she takes on a bet to
    get him elected student body president"— Provided by publisher.
Identifiers: LCCN 2023024518 | ISBN 9781250897466 (hardcover)
Subjects: CYAC: Friendship—Fiction. | Transgender people—Fiction. |
    Elections—Fiction. | Middle schools—Fiction. | Schools—Fiction.
Classification: LCC PZ7.1.H86419 Li 2024 | DDC [Fic]—dc23
LC record available at https://lccn.loc.gov/2023024518

First edition, 2024
Book design by L. Whitt
Feiwel and Friends logo designed by Filomena Tuosto
Printed in the United States of America by Lakeside Book Company,
Harrisonburg, Virginia

ISBN 978-1-250-89746-6 (hardcover)

10 9 8 7 6 5 4 3 2 1

FOR MY STUDENTS,
WHO REMIND ME WHO I AM AND WHO I CAN BE

1

Linus

YOU NEVER GET A SECOND CHANCE AT A FIRST IMPRESSION. (UNLESS YOU MOVE TO A NEW STATE!)

I'm nervous. Not this-will-give-me-the-edge-I-need nervous. I'm-gonna-puke nervous. And puking would be a huge problem because I'm just about to walk into Doolittle Middle School for the first time. I keep fiddling with the friendship bracelet Olive tied to my backpack the day before I moved away from her and the rest of my life back in New York. Mom pulls the car up to the main entrance of the school, and my heart kicks into hyperdrive. I squeeze my backpack hard against my chest, pressing against my binder beneath my shirt and my budding boobs under that. It's the same green L.L.Bean backpack I've had forever. Well, not exactly the same. My parents got me a new one when I changed my name—because my old one had my old name embroidered in white thread that had turned gray over time. Now I've got a new green backpack with bright white thread. And even though I'm pretty sure no other eighth grader in the world has their name embroidered on their backpack, it was such a sweet thing for them to do that I really couldn't . . . not use it. Even though I kind of didn't want to.

Linus. That's what the white thread says. That's me.

"Here we are," Mom says. Even though we've been here for like a full minute.

"Yeah. I guess I'd . . ." My voice trails off. I mean, we both know what's going to happen. I'm going to get out of this car, walk into the brick building, exist for six hours, and then . . . well, let's just make sure I make it to 2:30. Or, I guess, technically 2:32, according to the schedule printout the school sent me over the summer. The schedule I've worried to tatters.

"I'll be right here to pick you up after school, okay?"

I nod.

"And then we're going to head over to Grandma's, all right? I think we're going to do dinners with her on Mondays and Fridays."

I nod again. But I don't move.

"Do you want me to come in with you?" Mom goes to unbuckle her seat belt and my heart slams against my chest, beating against my ribs at an alarming rate.

"No!" I say, a little too loud. A little too forceful. Except maybe it's not too much of anything because, to be completely clear, the idea of *my mom* walking me to class on *my first day of eighth grade* is high-key horrifying.

Mom pulls her hand away from the buckle, but my heart doesn't quite return to normal. The image of her waving at me cheerfully through the doorway of a classroom as I sit down to learn algebra is still flooding my brain.

"Do you want a hug?" she asks after a moment.

This time my response comes less immediately to me. I'm not sure if the answer is supposed to be "Yes, of course I want to hug you! You're my mom, and I'm never too old for hugs!" or "Ugh, I'm a teen, and I'd rather die." I settle for giving her a pained grimace.

She laughs. "Say no more!"

I really wish I could stall a bit longer, but according to my schedule, civics class starts at 8:10, and it's 8:06 right now. And I literally have no idea where I'm going. Other than, you know, inside.

"Okay. Bye, Mom. Love you."

"Love you too, Liney."

I push open the door, and the world that was muffled behind the glass car window is suddenly sharp and insistent. And hot. Sure, early fall in the city can still be hot and gross, but a part of me thought things might be different in the Midwest. Apparently, the start of a new school year in Ohio can also be really hot. I think about closing the door, retreating to the cool and quiet car interior, but I'm pretty sure everyone is staring at me. The new boy. So I push through the I'm-almost-gonna-puke feeling and move toward the front door.

The sound of my shoes hitting the shiny blue floor echoes as I walk in. Am I walking too slowly? Should I look more excited? Am I too bouncy now? Is that off-putting? Should I stand up more? Will that make my boobs push out, even though I'm wearing a binder? Can people see the lines of my binder under my shirt? Will I have to explain that I really am a boy? Will I have to explain it again later after I've already told them? Am I standing like a boy? How do boys stand? Am I . . . My mind won't settle down.

Before this past year, I never really noticed my nerves. Or, at least, they never seemed to get in the way of things. When I was younger, my nerves made my ears turn pink, which no one really noticed because I had long hair. I guess the stuff I used to be nervous about was different too. Like . . . will I score a goal in the soccer game? Or . . . will Viola Bee make fun of me for giving her a beach towel for her birthday? (My mom made me do it.) That stuff is different than *Will people like me?* I guess it's not just *will* people like me. It's will *anyone?*

This kind of nervousness really started to kick in when I came out to my parents as trans last year. At the time, I mistakenly believed that coming out would just be a one-and-done event. Hurray! I'm a boy! Everyone is on board!

Not everyone was on board.

Because I kept having to tell people. My teachers. My soccer team. My friends. My friends' parents. I kept having to go into it.

Once I told people, they were really supportive. I mean it. Some people hugged me. Some people cried. Some people shrugged like it was no big deal. Only one person said, "I knew it!" But the whole thing was just exhausting. I feel like I spent the whole fall of seventh grade telling people I'm a boy. And the whole winter recovering from telling them. I backed away from a bunch of stuff—stopped playing soccer, stayed home during school dances, and slept through the weekends.

And, even though I tried to avoid the places where people might mess up, throughout the spring, months after I told everyone, even when they had the best of intentions, they still made mistakes.

They forgot my name. "Sorry! Old habit!"

Or to use my pronouns. "You're the same person to me!"

Or they'd do other, slightly strange, things. "Oh my god, I almost said you were going into the wrong bathroom!"

They would smile. And I would smile.

Kind of.

Anyway, now I'm at a new school. And I don't have to come out. I'm a boy here. And after a year of telling everyone and resting after telling everyone and living through everyone's mistakes, I'm ready to just be a boy. And to, I dunno, maybe do some stuff beyond homework for the first time in a year.

At least, that's what I told myself last night as I packed up my backpack and laid out my clothes—and by clothes, I mean my favorite T-shirt. It's got a Venn diagram on it. In one circle, there's a beaver playing the guitar. In the other, there's a duck playing a keyboard. And in the middle: a duck-billed platypus playing the keytar. I chose it because when I catch myself in the mirror and I'm wearing it, I always see the shirt first and crack up. Before I get too caught up in worrying about the way I look. Or the way others see me.

I make my way through another set of doors and into a large corridor.

"Hi, you must be Linus," says an adult—maybe a teacher or something? She's coming out of an office area. Was I supposed to stop in there?

"Uh, yeah. How did you know?" I ask.

"Well, it's a pretty small school. And you're the only new eighth grader!" She smiles, which I imagine is supposed to be comforting, but her words are the opposite of comforting. The *only* new eighth grader? I just want to *be*. I don't want to stand out! "I'm Ms. Hill." She reaches her hand toward me, and I shake it tentatively.

"I'm Linus. As you know." I give her one of those smiles where I don't show my teeth. The I'm-being-a-good-sport-but-I-kinda-hate-this smile.

"Hi, Linus. I'm the school counselor. I'm going to bring you to your first class."

Crap. No! Under no circumstances are we doing this.

"Uh, well, I feel, um, pretty confident!" I start to walk. Away. I try not to notice how the other students are looking at me. Eyeing the new boy and the overly friendly school counselor.

"Are you sure? I'm happy to help!"

"Yeah, totally. Love that. I'm just—"

And I run. I mean, I jog. I'm not really a runner. But I'm definitely a get-away-from-this-er.

As I careen around the corridor, I slam into another person. Hard to say if crashing into one of my new class-mates is more embarrassing than the school counselor touring me around the school on my first day.

The girl I crashed into has green hair. And she growls at me.

Okaaaaaay. This is worse.

2
Etta

ANYONE WHO WISHES THEY WERE YOUNG AGAIN FORGOT ABOUT MIDDLE SCHOOL.

Middle school is like a horror movie. Or maybe not, because I actually *like* horror movies. But I've been back in this school for less than five minutes, and I already hate it. Whoever this is practically dislocating my shoulder from running into me is just the icing on the cake. He goes to help me pick up my books, but I don't want help. I don't *need* help. I wave him away.

"Sorry!" The boy's voice is kind of breathy. I haven't seen him before. I don't think. Not that I care.

"Yeah." That's all I've got. My mom likes to say I'm in my monosyllabic period. Kind of like how Picasso had his blue period and Harry Styles had his boy band period. Except my monosyllable period is unlikely to result in great art. And my mom doesn't mean the phrase nicely. I can tell she's desperate for me to say more to her. About literally anything. Which makes me less likely to do it.

I grunt as I lean down to pick up my books from

the floor, and when I get back up, I'm not expecting the Mayor of Slamtown to still be gaping at me.

"Um, sorry," he says. Again.

"You said that." Wow. He got a full sentence out of me. Impressive.

"Yeah. This apology is for something else. I need . . . I need help getting to—"

He looks down at a worn printout of a student schedule. It looks old. I remember doing this project in fifth grade where the teacher had us write a letter from a fictional soldier to their family back home. We got extra credit if we "aged" the letter. You know, if we bathed it in tea and burned the edges, and used some swoopy font instead of Times New Roman or whatever. I wrote a love letter as a lesbian soldier to my fictional girlfriend from a future postapocalyptic war zone. It didn't go over well. Anyway, this kid's schedule looks like the other kids' letters from that class. Stained and folded over and over again.

"Do you know where that is?"

Shoot. He's been talking and I've been thinking about my fifth-grade history project. I lean over to look at the paper and cover my lack of attention.

A Period: Civics 8 (Mr. Todd) Room 2007

I pull out my phone, which I know I'm not supposed to use, but I'm a rebel like that, and check the screenshot of my own schedule. Identical words shine back at me.

"We're going to the same place." I sigh. "Follow me."

I start walking, my Doc Martens clomping as I make my way to the stairs leading to the 2000s classrooms.

"I'm Linus, by the way. I'm new."

I think about saying I don't care. But that seems harsh. And no one is watching. No need to be a total jerk.

"I'm Etta." I take a beat. "I'm old."

"Like an old soul or an old vampire trapped in the body of an eighth grader?"

I stop and look at Linus, who turns the brightest shade of red imaginable. Like, I don't know if neon red is a thing, but if it is, this is it. Aside from his tomato complexion, Linus is pretty unremarkable. He's taller than me. And a little heavier. Under his blush his skin is pale, and his hair is brownish reddish and floofs up from his head in an explosion of curls.

"Sorry," he says.

"You keep saying that."

"Well, the first one was for knocking into you. The second was for asking for help. And the third is for being weird." Linus runs his hand through his already floofy hair.

I think for a second, and then say, "I only accept the second one."

Linus blinks, then says, "Okay."

"The vampire thing was actually pretty funny."

"You didn't laugh."

"I'm not a laugher." Truer words were never spoken. I mean, maybe I used to be a laugher, but not now. Not since . . . Well, everyone says that middle school sucks. And they're right. Let's leave it at that.

Next year, though, there's a chance that things will change. While everyone else funnels into the local public school, I'll be making my way to Nova, an alternative high school that occupies a revamped office building downtown. Nova has been on my radar ever since my brother got in three years ago. He went there for a year, bailed, and headed over to Higgins High. Of course Jamie would get the chance of a lifetime to go to school at Nova and then say, "Thanks but no thanks!" And it *is* a chance. Getting into Nova is not a given. And to have a shot, I need to, you know, finish middle school and come up with a compelling application. It's pretty much the only reason I'm here at school and literally not anywhere else.

"Okay. Too cool to laugh. Got it. Maybe we can come up with a hand signal? Like a physical version of laughter that isn't laughter? But that lets me know that you get my jokes."

What is this kid asking about? A hand signal? "Like a thumbs-up?"

"Sure. If you're into that."

I think about it. The idea of giving a thumbs-up goes against my carefully crafted vibe. "I'm not," I say.

"Oh. That's okay." Linus smiles shyly. Or maybe it's a nervous smile. I wonder what I look like to him. With my green hair, my foundation that makes my skin a full shade paler than it already is, my thick stay-away-from-me eyeliner, and my spiky choker, I'm sure I don't really read as a thumbs-up kind of gal.

But something about the way Linus is smiling is so sweet it makes me start to consider what hand gesture I might be willing to do to let him know I get his jokes. "How about this?" I say, lifting my hand palm down and tilting it from side to side.

"That's more of an 'eh' gesture. And, let's be honest, I'm gonna be saying some pretty hilarious things." Linus raises his eyebrows and grimaces.

I do the gesture.

"Are you saying that comment was funny?"

I respond in a deadpan voice. "It's hilarious that you think you're hilarious." After about two seconds, I crack a grin. Linus gives me an enthusiastic thumbs-up. A part of me hates to admit it, but it's fun talking to him.

"Aren't we gonna be late?"

"Eh, it's day one. How many of those opening ice-breakers teachers like to torture us with are absolutely essential?"

Linus's eyebrows pinch together, and I can tell being later than he has to be is making him uncomfortable. I sigh and start walking again.

"Don't get used to me being this useful," I mutter. It sounds like what I should say at this moment. Something cutting.

Linus laughs, and even though I want to hate that he's laughing at me being unapproachable, I can't. He's . . . so sweet. Like a golden retriever. And I can't hate a golden retriever. Or any dog for that matter. We make our way out of the stairwell, into the hallway, and down to room 2007. School isn't *so* terrible, I guess. I can go through the motions. At least until I get to Nova.

And then I walk into civics.

There are two open seats.

And both of them are next to Marigold Stimpson.

Crap.

3

Linus

IT WOULD BE REALLY GREAT IF I COULD PULL OFF A SUCCESSFUL INTERACTION WITH A PEER THIS MORNING!

I really hope no one is expecting me to remember anything from this first class, 'cause it's a blur. Despite Etta's comment, we aren't lucky enough to miss the icebreakers. In fact, the entirety of the class period seems to be dedicated to them. Not very much of it seems to have anything to do with civics. I don't even really know what "civics" is. I do appreciate that Mr. Todd has clear rules and instructions. There's no free-range interactions. Everything is scripted. Which means there really aren't many ways to mess up. Thank goodness. Because if there are ways to mess things up, I'm going to be thinking about them. Even if the chances of me doing the messing up are slim to none, I'm still thinking about it. Almost always.

So now I'm sitting at my desk, making what Mr. Todd calls a contour drawing, where you basically just have to stare at another person and draw them while that same person is staring at you and drawing you. It's kind of awkward. But at least it seems awkward for everyone and not just me. I'm paired up with the girl next to me. The girl between me and Etta. I wish I was with Etta. But maybe it's okay that I'm getting to know someone else. I just wish the someone else didn't make me blush furiously while I draw her.

"Hey . . . Liiiiiiinus," says the blond girl. Her head is cocked to the side as she reads the name tent Mr. Todd had me make at the beginning of the class. Well, everyone else made them at the beginning of class. Etta and I made them when we got to class. Late.

"Hey . . ." I mimic her actions, tilting my head to read her name tent, "Mmmmmmarigold." There's a pause, and I furrow my brow to prepare for the "Wow, that was super not funny!" I'm about to get. I'm in real agony as the silence stretches between us. Sure, I slid by Etta with my odd sense of humor, but there's no way I'll go two for two on initial interactions. I swear, I really thought I was going to be able to start fresh and lay low at this new school, but here I am, busting out my awkward sense of humor first thing. Two times in a row.

I guess a tiger can't change its stripes. Or, rather, a Linus can't change his dad jokes. It's just not a choice I get to make. Like with being trans. When I told my grandma that I'm a boy, she said something like "Well, that's your choice." And maybe that was her way of supporting me. But all I could think at the time was, *It's not a choice. It's who I am.*

But then Marigold bursts out laughing. It's a bright sound. I look around to see if other people are staring at us. The only person who seems to notice is Etta, who gives me our *that's funny* hand gesture and then abruptly stops and slowly slashes her thumb across her throat. I guess that's our new sign for *That's absolutely not funny in any way, shape, or form; please stop embarrassing yourself.* Noted. Other than Etta, everyone else is wrapped up in their drawings. Thank goodness. Because they would probably ask why Marigold's laughing. And then I would have to explain the whole name-reading thing. Which, even though it's making Marigold laugh now, would absolutely be not-at-all funny when it's retold. But no one but Etta is even really paying attention to us. Even when Marigold snorts a little, midlaugh.

That snort brings my focus entirely back to her. And for this brief moment, the rest of the world falls away, and it's just me and Marigold sharing this strange laugh. There's a part of me that particularly likes that Marigold snorts when she laughs. Other than that, she seems to be almost *too* perfect. She's what Mom would call "a looker," which is just a tame way of saying "hot." But I try not to pay too much attention to that. Instead, I focus on her face. She has gray-green eyes, and there are freckles dotting the bridge of her nose, though it looks like she's tried to cover them with pale, almost-white concealer that's a few shades lighter than her skin. Those freckles are stubborn though. You can still see them peeking through her makeup. They're adorable.

Marigold is still laughing, so I join her. To, you know, be polite. But then I start coughing. And I can't stop. So I just keep coughing. Sputtering. I can't quite catch my breath. It's like I'm in some first-day-of-school nightmare. Except I'm wearing clothes. So at least there's that.

"Mr. Todd!" Marigold raises her hand, but doesn't wait to be called on. "I'm gonna take Linus to get some water. He can't stop coughing."

"Thank you, Marigold."

Marigold puts a hand on my elbow, and even though I'm still worrying about coughing for the entirety of eighth grade, there's this zippy feeling that shoots up my arm as she guides me to stand up and follow her out of the room. When we're in the hallway, my cough fades, but Marigold keeps her hand on my elbow. She's not pulling or dragging. Just guiding. I try not to freak out about her touching me. At least, I try not to freak out on the outside. Inside, there's a volcanic eruption of freaking out. And I'm kind of liking it?

When we get to the water fountain, I lean down and silently lament that no one has invented a cool way to drink out of one of these things.

"So, you're new here . . . ," Marigold says as I finish my slurping and lift my head from the stream of water.

"Yep," I say, wiping off my mouth in what I hope is a semi-smooth way. It's a futile hope. I know it.

"And you're from . . . ?"

"Um, my family just moved here from New York."

"Why would you move *here*?" She kind of scoffs when she says the word *here*, but her eyes have this look of genuine interest. I can feel the tips of my ears getting hot.

And, I mean . . . I get it. I wondered the same thing when my parents told me we were moving from New York to Ohio. Ohio is about as Middle America as you get. We moved here because of my grandma—the one who thinks being trans is a choice. Anyway, she fell a few months ago, and Mom has work that can be done from anywhere, so we moved to the Midwest to spend more time with her. Which . . . I mean, I love Grandma, but I don't really *need* more time with her, exactly.

But I don't want to get into all of that with Marigold, so I say, "Uh, shouldn't we get back to—"

"Oh, it's fine. Mr. T knows what's up."

I have this moment where two feelings collide in my body. On the one hand, I'm kind of excited that Marigold isn't eager to end our time together. And maybe that means that we might be friends or something. My brain is kind of going into hyperdrive about what *or something* might entail. And on the other hand, I was already *late* to civics class. Can I really afford to miss half the first day of class because I'm getting water? Sure, I'm getting water with a cute girl, but still! I settle for a sheepish "Well, I don't. And I want to, uh, make a decent impression on my first day."

"No, of course. Of course! You're new. You're doing a great job." She gives me an *okay* sign with her hand, and I'm standing taller. My chest swells up—not in a big-boobs way, in an I'm-proud way.

"Thanks," I say.

Marigold looks surprised at my words, but she shakes it off and asks, "Do you have a phone?" I reflexively move my hand near the pocket of my jeans. Marigold's eyes follow the movement. "Great." She holds her palm out expectantly. I don't really feel comfortable handing her, or anyone, my phone. There's a lot of personal stuff on it—particularly photos of me before I came out. Not that I think Marigold would, like, hack my phone right in front of me. But still. It's like a piece of me.

"You can just tell me," I say. I look over my shoulder. Mom explained to me that phones aren't allowed at my new school, but we agreed that I could hold on to mine in case of an emergency. She didn't say what the emergency might be, but we both knew. Living while trans anywhere comes with its own risks.

And, like, maybe an emergency could involve

needing Marigold's phone number at some point? It would be foolish, reckless even, *not* to accept her offer at this moment. Right?

Marigold recites her number, and I plug it into my contacts and then send her a text with a frog emoji.

"The frog is from me," I say.

"You're so weird." I'm not quite sure how to take that, but she's smiling at least. So there's that. I try not to overthink her observation, but my brain is going a mile a minute imagining how *weird* could be the best possible thing to be and also how it could be the absolute worst.

We get back to the classroom just as Mr. Todd is talking about the elections for student council.

"Nominations are due on Tuesday, after the long Labor Day weekend, then you'll all be able to participate in the Q&A session during assembly on Wednesday. And then, of course, there's elections for president, which you eighth graders are finally eligible for. We'll be sharing more details at the school assembly this week."

I let out a sigh of relief. At least I didn't miss anything super important.

"I really want you all to consider this. Student government has the ability to change your lives at school." Mr. Todd is speaking earnestly, the way teachers like to talk sometimes. I feel kind of bad that I'm not more into it, but student council isn't really my thing.

I'm pretty sure it's not really Etta's thing either,

because I hear some kind of annoyed sigh come from the other side of Marigold. Even though we got along pretty well, she comes across as the kind of person who's pretty over it. I'm not sure what *it* is. But folks like Etta want nothing to do with it.

As everyone starts packing up (even though the bell hasn't rung yet), I pull my schedule out of my pocket. English is listed next. I wonder if I have that with Marigold too. Or Etta. Etta's probably the safer person to initiate secondary contact with. I'm just about to ask her, but as soon as the bell rings, she jumps out of her chair like she's been electrocuted and bolts toward the door, her worn messenger bag slamming against her leg.

I guess I'll have to figure out another way to get to English.

4
Etta

I THOUGHT MIDDLE SCHOOL WAS BAD ALREADY, BUT IT'S IMPOSSIBLY WORSE WHEN YOU HAVE TO ATTEND IT WITH YOUR EX–BEST FRIEND.

I hate Marigold Stimpson.

Mom doesn't like it when I use the word *hate*. She says it's a loaded word, and I should be careful about the language I use.

But I *am* being careful about my language. Because I know that what I feel toward Marigold Stimpson is hate.

Maybe it's because I cared about her. And because I think she used to care about me. That's what best friends are supposed to do. Care about each other. Maybe even love each other.

And I know what we have now is the polar opposite.

Ex-friend + Ex-care = Hate

I honestly don't know what happens in class. Mr. Todd isn't, like, a terrible human, but he's trying so hard to be enthusiastic and build a "positive class culture" or whatever that it's honestly embarrassing. I think about asking to go to the bathroom, but I don't want Marigold to think she has any power over me anymore. So I just sit.

In agony.

And relive my three interactions with Marigold from the summer.

For fifty minutes.

Interaction #1: It's the end of the last day of school. The first moment of summer. Marigold and I are hugging and jumping up and down, screaming about how seventh grade is over. We spent so much of the year lamenting that we might not survive. And we did it! We talk about spending as much time together this summer as possible. But, first, Marigold has a trip for the first week of summer. She promises to text me every day until she gets back on Saturday.

Interaction #2: I text Marigold every day. She doesn't text me back. I wonder if maybe she doesn't have cell service. Or if things with her family got busy. So I wait. And I send her messages about everything and nothing. On Saturday, she finally texts. I think we should take a break from being friends.

Interaction #3: I show up on Marigold's porch and beg her to talk to me about her text. Beg her to be my friend again. Tell her I will do anything. Her parents call my mom and have her pick me up.

By the time class is finally ending, I've relived those three interactions 7.333333 (repeating) times. When the bell rings, I'm out of there. Getting as far away from Marigold Stimpson and her perfect-smelling shampoo as quickly as I possibly can.

I swat away the hot, insistent tear that's trailing down my face as I book it to art class. Can't have weak tears smudging my eyeliner and making anyone think I might care about anything that happens in middle school.

After our three start-of-summer interactions, Marigold ghosted me completely. Never heard from her again. Absolutely savage. Over the summer, I did two things. I cried a lot about Marigold, and I got really into horror movies. For some reason, horror movies were the only thing that could help me forget that Marigold had broken me. Fear felt better than sadness. And after a while, the movies didn't even scare me anymore. I just kind of got obsessed with how they worked. The special effects. The way the scripts were structured. It all fascinated me. And when I wasn't watching horror movies, I was crying. I cried trying to understand. Trying to figure out what I could do. Trying to figure out how I could change. And, to be honest, I thought I cried so much that I didn't have any tears left. Especially not for terrible Marigold Stimpson.

But apparently, now I have different kinds of tears. And I hate them. So I spend all of art class turning into a block of ice. A block of ice doesn't hurt. Not when someone tells it that she doesn't want to be its best friend.

Or friend at all. Not when it misses that someone. And certainly not when that same someone sits next to it for fifty minutes of civics class.

And a block of ice doesn't cry. 'Cause, like, tears are water. So they're frozen.

By the time lunch rolls around, I've convinced myself that it might be worth talking to Marigold. I'm a block of ice now. She can't hurt me. And maybe she can explain why things changed. Especially when they used to be kind of great. We grew up on the same road, Piccadilly Circle, which meant we spent practically every hour that wasn't in school at each other's houses. In fifth grade, we got really into rom-coms and started a tradition of watching a new one every weekend night. Bonus points for Hallmark originals. I'm not much of a rom-com person, but with Marigold? Back then? It was fun. It was silly. It was wonderful. So to lose that? It just feels wrong.

In the cafeteria, I skip past the line and walk up to the kitchen door.

"Etta! My favorite customer!" Ms. Hannah, the lunch supervisor, pulls a bagged lunch from her cart and hands it to me. "No meat. No eggs. No dairy. The lentil soup should be good for you too!" She's so cheerful as she runs through the menu and reminds me what I can and can't eat.

"Thanks," I mumble when she finishes her spiel.

"See you tomorrow?" She always asks that.

And I always smile and shrug.

I find an empty spot and fish through my bag. I move the contents around. I'm not exactly hungry, but Mom says my body is bad at giving me hunger cues, so I have to eat something during meal times. I pull out an apple and start chewing.

"Etta!" A voice calls out from a few tables down. I look around, and there's Linus. Sweet, golden retriever Linus. I honestly had kind of forgotten about him with all the Marigold drama and the freezing and whatnot.

And, speaking of Marigold, there she is. Next to Linus.

I give him a wave. Well, it's more of a salute. I mouth, "I'm good," even though I'm anything but. Linus's eyebrows draw together. Then I wave Marigold over. I feel sort of guilty. I don't want to leave Linus alone on his first day, but I also don't really want to talk about my friend breakup with him sitting right there.

Marigold doesn't make a move at first, so Linus just looks between the two of us like a lost puppy. *Sorry, kiddo, Mom and Dad are fighting.* Then *Linus* goes to stand up. Like maybe he's going to move over to my table with Marigold. But she puts a hand on his shoulder and says something to him. He gives her a concerned look, but then he settles back in his seat as she gets up and walks toward me.

Sure, I'm the one who waved her over, but I think about running.

Again.

Instead, I work to stay frozen.

"Hey, Etta."

"Hey," I say.

"Look, I know things got kinda messed up this summer . . ."

Ice. Ice. I'm a block of ice. I start digging into my lunch bag again. I don't really care about you, Marigold. Just looking for some answers. Definitely not noticing that you have squeaky clean Air Force 1s on your feet for the first day of school. Nope. Not noticing at all. And I'm definitely not thinking about our weekly sleepovers where we would make so many friendship bracelets that our wrists literally couldn't hold any more. And I'm not looking at my own wrists now and noticing how pale and bare they look. And how you seem to have filled your wrists with new bracelets.

"Messed up doesn't even begin to cover it," I mumble. "Look, I just wanted to—"

She cuts me off. "But I think that . . . Look, I've been thinking about it, and I wanted to let you know that I'm gonna be applying to Nova."

What? My ice starts to melt. Nova is *my* thing. Marigold knows that. We used to talk about it. Before. And now it's after. And I get to have *my* things. She's got everything. She's got all her friends. And her basketball team. And her leads in the school musical. She doesn't get *this*.

"Excuse me?" I hiss, trying to keep my voice down.

"I thought it was only fair to tell you. But, like, this doesn't have anything to do with *you*." She looks away, like this conversation is boring and she wants to find something better to talk about. Or someone better to talk to.

There's something about her casualness that makes my blood boil. And boiling blood and ice? Those two things don't play well together. "Like hell!" I'm not yelling. But . . . the sound that comes out of my mouth *feels* like a yell. If I were in some kind of horror movie with a paranormal twist, this is where my powers would show up. I'd give Marigold a bloody nose with my mind. Or create a localized earthquake in the Doolittle cafeteria. But this isn't a paranormal horror movie. It's my life. So, instead, I can only say, "You wouldn't even know about Nova if it weren't for me." Sure, for a while we had talked about trying to both get in—and about how if one of us got in but not the other, we wouldn't hold it against each other. But that was *before*.

"Well, *that's* not true," Marigold says dismissively.

"You certainly wouldn't have thought about it twice."

"What can I say? You really talked the program up. I looked into it, and it seems like a really good option."

Something in me turns desperate, and without my consent, my voice turns whiny. "Marigold. Seriously. You know they only take a few kids from each school. And . . ." *And I was really hoping to get away from you next year. I really need this.* I don't say those words. But I think them.

"Look, I know that you're, like, a wannabe Wednesday Addams who is anti-everything or whatever, but maybe Nova isn't going to be into that. Maybe they'll want people who actually, like, care about school. Did you ever think about that?"

She stands up to walk back to her table. Back to Linus, who is looking at me with that confused expression.

My heart starts to sputter in my chest, beating against my ribs in a weird, awkward rhythm. I think about those friendship bracelets, about how Marigold managed to end our friendship and find dozens of others. Me? I'm a loner. And even though part of me wants to think it's a choice on my part, there's this whisper of doubt that says that it isn't. That no one *wants* to be my friend. The Marigolds of the world get friends.

Marigold gets everything.

But she doesn't get this.

And she's not going to get Linus either.

The era of Marigold Stimpson getting whatever she wants is over.

5

Linus

DINNER + GRANDMA = TRANS PANIC!

Despite managing to make two friends on the first day at Doolittle, I am in Mom's car by 2:33.

"How was school, Liney?"

"Exhausting!" I huff, and indicate impatiently that we should leave.

"You up for seeing your grandmother?"

The answer is no. I'm not up for it. I'm never up for it. Especially not after battling through day one of eighth grade. However, it is clear that in this particular case, there is a correct answer.

"Yeah. Sure." I slide my phone out and think about texting Marigold, since I have her number now. Which is kind of amazing when you think about it! I start blushing and hope Mom doesn't notice.

"You texting with Olive?" Mom asks, side-eyeing me.

Shoot! I forgot that I promised Olive I would give her a rundown as soon as school ended.

"Yeah," I lie as I pull up my text thread with Olive

and start furiously typing. My phone rings a moment after I hit send on my first text. "It's Olive," I tell Mom.

"Oh, put her on speaker!"

I think about not doing it. Because I just want to talk to Olive and not talk to Olive and *my mom*. But, again, there's clearly a right answer here. I use the screen at the front of Mom's car to pipe in Olive through our speakers.

"Hey, Olive you!" I say, putting some more enthusiasm into my voice for our typical greeting than I truly feel. *Olive you* is a play on the fact that the letters in *Olive* spell "I Love" if you switch the vowels. I've opened every conversation with Olive this way ever since we figured that out in first grade.

"Linus! First day of school! How was it? Was it great?"

"Hi, Olive. You're on speakerphone," Mom chips in.

"Hi, Ms. Stout! Linus, I'm dying over here. HOW DID IT GO?"

I laugh, reenergized by Olive's demanding tone, and launch into a blow-by-blow of the day. How I ran into Etta in the hallway, and even though she might have seemed a little intimidating at first, she was, in fact, really helpful. How I made friends with Marigold (though I don't really get into the fact that I think I have a crush on her). How lunch at Doolittle is pretty good, all things considered.

"Do you think you'll join the soccer team or something?" Olive asks. "You were always really good at soccer."

"Yeah, but I've never played on a boys' team," I hedge.

"Might be worth trying," Olive says.

"I agree with Olive," Mom adds. I give her a please-stop-talking look. She smiles at me and mimes zipping her lips.

"We'll see . . . ," I say. There's just so many ways that joining the soccer team could go wrong.

"I thought you said you wanted to try doing more things. Get back into everything."

I *did* say that. Just before I left, when I was trying to get over how mad I was that we were moving, Olive and I had a big conversation where she decided that all we needed to do was "reframe" the move. I didn't really know what she meant by that, but we ended up coming up with a list of things that could be good about moving to Ohio.

"You could always follow in my footsteps and run for student council." I can hear Olive's signature twinge of sarcasm. Olive has always been the more outgoing of the two of us. I had friends in New York because she and I were a package deal. That didn't change after I came out as a boy. Making speeches, hoping to make the world better, getting people to like you—that's all stuff Olive is really good at. Me? Not so much.

"Oh, shoot! Sorry, but my dad is calling me down-stairs. We'll text later, yeah?"

"Say hi to your dads for me," says Mom.

"Bye, Olive!"

I spend the rest of the ride home thinking about texting Marigold. And then thinking about if I *did* get the courage to text Marigold, what would the best, funniest, and most suave text be?

I don't, in fact, ending up texting Marigold anything.

━━

According to my parents, there are a lot of reasons we moved from New York to Ohio. But the big reason that trumps all the others is my grandmother.

At least that's the big reason for my parents. Things with my grandmother post-transition aren't super smooth. So, the closer we get to her house, the more I steel myself, rehearsing the words I'll say when she inevitably messes up my name. My pronouns.

I think about bringing it up to Mom. Mentioning that it would be great if she could speak up and help with getting Grandma to adjust her language, but I stop myself. It feels like a lot to ask.

We turn into Grandma's gravel driveway, and I suck in my breath and close my eyes.

"Hi, Mom," Mom sings out as she opens the storm door. "I've got Linus with me! And Doug should be coming over in a bit."

"Doug and Linus!" Grandma repeats from the kitchen. I let out my breath and follow Mom into the house. At least she got it right once. "I've made waffles, including Mickey-shaped ones. I know breakfast for dinner is your favorite!"

"Thanks, Grandma," I say, giving her my best smile. She's trying. I mean, sure, it's three o'clock, hardly dinnertime. And I haven't had a Mickey waffle since I was six. As we set the table, we go through an abbreviated version of my day for Grandma. I leave out a lot. And I try to stop talking sometimes. But then I look at my grandmother, and she purses her lips and tilts her head. I'm not sure if that's her way of asking me to share more or her way of saying she doesn't know how to respond. Regardless, I keep tacking on odd details about my first day and inwardly cringing. I don't talk about Marigold because if my grandmother is awkward about her grandchild being trans, then there is a nonzero chance she'll have an aneurysm if I tell her that I have a crush on a girl.

Dad gets there about halfway through the interminable breakfast-for-not-quite-dinner starring Linus's awkward stories about his first day of school.

"Hey, Dad!" Do I sound *too* relieved to have someone else here? Is that rude? I'm not sure I care if it's rude at this point.

"Hey, Linus, how's the new school?"

I groan.

"You've already had to do the report a couple of times, eh?"

"Yeah." I start ticking off my fingers. "Olive, Mom, Grandma—" My phone vibrates in my pocket, so I excuse myself to go to the bathroom.

There's a message from Marigold.

There's a message from *Marigold*!

I try not to freak out as I slide the notification open.

> **Marigold:** Linus! So cool to meet you today. Do you remember if there was civics homework?

I mean, sure, asking if there's homework isn't exactly grade-A flirting, but she texted *me* about homework. Not her (I assume) millions of other friends. *Me!* Doolittle's only new eighth grader.

I fumble as I text back and struggle to remember what our civics teacher—was his name Mr. Todd?—said at the end of class.

> **Me:** No. Mr. Todd said something about student council, I think?
>
> **Marigold:** Oh, yeah. I think I might try that!

Reading that text, I think for a fleeting moment that it might be kind of nice to be on student council. Particularly if Marigold is also a part of it. I mean, having a reason to spend time together would be kind of great. Because I would really *like* to spend more time with her. I'm not sure how to do that without the built-in structure of a school-organized activity. But, then again, if that school activity is student council, maybe I would be biting off more than I can chew? If I'm nervous walking into my first day of eighth grade, imagine how petrified I'd be giving a speech to the entire class.

It's not like I have to decide right now. What I do have to do right now is think of something cool to say to Marigold in response to her text. I settle on:

Me: Oh, cool!

Did I really think I would ever be able to pull off suave in a text?

Marigold: Do you think you might try it?

I'm really not sure how to take this. Is this an invitation? Like "We should do this together"? Or small talk? "I don't know what to type, so here's something"? Or . . . or . . . My mind floods with a million ways to take Marigold's question. And absolutely zero answers to said question.

Me: Not sure.

This might be the worst text exchange known to man. It's hard to know for sure.

Marigold: See you tomorrow!

Okay. Seeing you tomorrow is good. Seeing you tomorrow means that she might *want* to see me tomorrow.

"Linus, everything okay in there, tiger?" Dad calls from the table.

"Yeah, just . . ." I don't really know what to say. I would like a little more time to freak out about Marigold Last-Name-Currently-Unknown texting me. "I'm pooping!"

"Linus!"

"We don't need a play-by-play, tiger."

"You asked!" I yell back.

I flush the toilet (even though I didn't use it) and wash my hands (even though I didn't really do anything) and head back toward the table.

And that's when I hear my grandmother.

"How's the transition going for her?" she asks my parents. I freeze. I think about running to the table and telling her to ask *me* how I'm transitioning. And questioning what she means by *transition*. And demanding that she use my proper pronouns. But I wait, hoping that Mom or Dad will say something.

"Oh, you know, it's still early."

No dice from Dad.

"And, well, you know, it's a lot to get used to. But we'll all figure it out."

And a strikeout from Mom.

I mean, *they* don't misgender me in their responses. But they don't correct Grandma. Guilty by association.

I clear my throat and walk back into the dining room.

"Oh, hey, we were just talking about you!" Mom says.

I think about saying something bold. Something like, "No, you weren't." I'd be calm but firm. I'd spell out the facts. I'd say, "Grandma asked how the transition is going for *her*," and I would remind them that I'm not *her*.

But that response and the uncomfortable conversation that would follow stays in my head. I don't want to get into a fight. And getting into a fight definitely isn't the *right* thing to do at dinner with my grandmother. So, instead, I weakly joke, "Oh, anything interesting?"

Dad chuckles and Mom awkwardly segues into plans to take Grandma to a movie later in the week. I press my lips together and bite down to pull my attention away from my family. From the way my parents didn't correct my grandmother. From my own thoughts.

But my thoughts are pretty insistent. I think back to talking to Etta and Marigold. It felt so easy. They didn't squint at me, trying to figure out which parts of my face still look like a girl's. They didn't think twice about what pronouns to use. They just accepted me.

I feel my phone buzz in my pocket. Is it another text from Marigold? What would Marigold say if I told her about all of this?

I sneak my phone out under the table because I'm incapable of waiting to see if Marigold has texted again. Olive's name flashes across the screen, and I feel bad because I'm disappointed.

"Linus, no phones at the table," Dad says before I can slide open the text thread.

"Right," I say, and shove my phone back into my pocket.

6
Etta

IN WHICH I NEED TO COME UP WITH A WAY TO BEEF UP MY NOVA APP. STAT.

Starting school at 8:10 is bad enough without also having to cram into the auditorium with three hundred of your least favorite not-friends for an assembly. Mr. Todd is on the stage, raising his hand and asking students to raise their hands and close their mouths. A few kids—especially the sixth graders (poor, naive babies)—do what he asks. I absolutely do not.

I look for Linus but can't find him. When Marigold walks through the door, I look away as fast as humanly possible and slump in my seat. I seriously might have whiplash.

As we wait for everyone to settle, I think about Marigold's last words to me at lunch on the first day of school. The ones that have been running through my head constantly: *Look, I know that you're, like, a wannabe Wednesday Addams who is anti-everything or whatever, but maybe Nova isn't going to be into that. Maybe they'll want people who actually, like, care about school.*

And even though I really, really want Marigold to be wrong, the fact that I *cannot* stop thinking about it has me worried she might be right. I need to have *something* to list on my application under *extracurriculars*. I sneak out my phone and pull up the Nova website. A black-and-white photo of a group of three students and a teacher all talking animatedly is splashed across the home page. None of the kids in the picture look exactly *popular*. They look normal. Well, normal-ish. Maybe a bit weird. But happy too. Weird and happy. Isn't that what I want to be? And isn't Nova the way to get there? A window pops up inviting interested students to attend an open house. I shoot a quick text to Mom and Jamie asking if someone can give me a ride.

Jamie responds almost instantly.

Jamie: ride a bike

I roll my eyes and start typing a cutting response. Something that would really annoy my older brother. But Mom's text rolls in and diffuses my no-doubt scathing reply (sure, I haven't thought of anything yet, but I would have!).

Mom: We'll figure it out!

"Welcome back, students. I hope you are feeling more settled after a couple days of school." There's a smattering of claps. Cyrus Cheslak stands and keeps slow-clapping well past when the meager applause has ended. Could eighth-grade boys be any more obnoxious? My eyes cut over to Marigold, who is sitting next to Linus. I swear I didn't watch as she found her seat in the second row. It's just hard not to notice her white-blond hair. She leans over and whispers something to Linus. I guess it's not just eighth-grade boys who are obnoxious. It's all eighth graders.

Except maybe Linus.

"Ms. Frost asked me to speak to you today about student council." Under normal circumstances, I would groan, but Marigold's words push to the front of my mind: *Maybe they'll want people who actually, like, care about school.* So I swallow my acerbic comment and listen. Because if I go out for student council, that would definitely show that I care about school. Maybe I still have a shot at Nova?

"Each grade will have four representatives." Okay, that's not bad. Instead of a one-in-a-million chance, it's a four-in-one-hundred chance. Way better odds. "We're looking for two boys and two girls for each grade. We want to keep things balanced. If you are interested, you'll do a question-and-answer session with your grade so they can make an informed decision about who they want representing them. And then we'll have a vote."

My heart sinks. A vote? Sure, I think that my school is mostly filled with sheep—obnoxious sheep—but I'm hardly a qualified shepherd. It's hard to imagine them voting for *me*.

"After that, our eighth-grade reps will be eligible to apply to be student council president. If more than one person applies, we'll have school-wide election. Any questions?"

A smattering of hands go up. I sink into my seat. Sure, for a brief moment, I thought I might be able to add *student council* to my Nova app, but it's looking like that might not be a real possibility.

The assembly drones on. I think about popping in my earbuds and tuning everything out. Instead, I cross my arms, and my mind (totally against my will!) runs through my conversation with Marigold. And every time I get to the part when she tells me she's going to apply to Nova, I get angrier.

When the assembly ends and students start to make their way to class, I stay in my seat, numb and unmoving. Out of the corner of my eye, I see Marigold march up from her spot in the second row to talk to Mr. Todd. She smiles and has her eyes open a little wider than normal, and she nods whenever he says anything.

Of course. Marigold's going to do student council. She's probably going to be president. Like she needs another way to beat me out for Nova. She finishes whatever meaningless conversation she's having with Mr. Todd and walks back toward the door. Toward me. And as she walks by, I mutter under my breath. I don't use words, exactly. But the sentiment is clear.

"Excuse me?" Marigold stops.

I don't say anything, but I feel a terrible smile form on my lips. Because she isn't just walking away. There's this sick part of me that's glad that I have some effect on her. If she were totally over our friendship, she would ignore me, or worse still, she wouldn't even notice me enough to ignore me. Instead, she's actually talking to me.

"What were you saying about student council?" She shifts her weight so that her hip sticks out.

I sigh. And I think about not saying anything. And then I think about saying something mean. Which is what I do.

"I said: Student council is a joke. Anyone can get elected because this school is full of predictable puppets who'll do whatever's popular. It's not, like, even real."

"You don't have to be salty just because you aren't popular," Marigold shoots back.

I look at Marigold's wrists with the friendship bracelets. She's right. I'm not popular. I start to feel my cheeks get hot. It's not my cheeks exactly. It's the space between my cheeks and my eyes. I'm worried that hot tears are about to spill out of my eyes, but I will them out of existence. Just because I'm not popular doesn't mean I'm powerless. It doesn't mean that I can't *do* something. Something that would really mess with Marigold's idea of what can happen at Doolittle and who gets to decide.

"I bet I could get anyone elected student council president if I really put my mind to it." The words are out before I can think them through.

They land. There's a moment of triumph when Marigold freezes and looks at me. Really looks at me. In a way she hasn't looked at me since the beginning of the summer. Like I'm someone who might have something interesting to say.

"So prove it." She sinks deeper into her hip.

"What?" I snort.

"I said *prove* it. If you're such a middle school mastermind who can get anyone elected, do it."

I smile, a plan already taking root and feeling surprisingly possible. The thought of winning this bet with Marigold feels *good*. And, let's be honest, good is something I haven't felt in months. I'm making a lightning-fast pro-and-con list in my brain, and it's decidedly lopsided:

Pro: Winning will shut Marigold up.

Pro: Winning will prove my point.

Pro: Winning will be something to put on my Nova application—winning campaign manager (and bonus, I don't have to run myself!).

"Fine," I say. There's a very real chance my smile is moving into creepy territory, visions of victory dancing across my mind. I slump back in my seat, trying to appear bored and aloof. I look at my nails. They're painted black to match, well, everything I'm currently wearing. And my soul. "Name someone."

Marigold crosses her arms across her chest and gives me a smirk as she says, "The new boy. Linus."

Okaaaaay. Maybe getting the new boy, aka Doolittle's awkward king rising, elected president is going to be more of a challenge than I was betting on.

7
Linus

I JUST WANT TO BE A REGULAR EIGHTH-GRADE BOY. REGULAR EIGHTH-GRADE BOYS DO <u>NOT</u> RUN FOR STUDENT COUNCIL!

My brain has been replaying dinner with Grandma—specifically the part when she misgendered me—on repeat. I know that I've chatted with Marigold and exchanged awkward jokes with Etta, but most of my brain has been thinking about how I should have said something. I try to shove the moment out of my mind. There's nothing I can do about it now. As I walk into civics class, Mr. Todd is standing in the doorway greeting students and handing out student council nomination forms. Or he's trying to hand them out. Not many people are biting. I'm certainly not. Even if I *was* considering joining something, like Olive and I talked about on the phone, the lack of interest on the part of almost every other kid in the class would keep me from accepting that sheet of paper. It's not that I'm so interested in the opinions of my peers or in following the crowd; it's more that I'm kind of enjoying just blending in. Sure, if there's something I really want to do, I'll do it. Probably. I mean, I would at least really strongly consider it. But student council? That might work for Olive, but it's just not my thing.

Marigold flounces into class late, and my heart does this weird thing where it sputters. Just a little. Just enough for me to notice. The other times I notice my heart sputtering kind of like this are when someone accidentally calls me by my old name. But this is different than that. More pleasant.

Telling my parents that I was trans was decidedly not pleasant. My heart wasn't just doing a sputter; it was pounding—slamming so hard that I thought my ribs might break.

I had explained that I'm a boy. That I wanted them to call me Linus and use he/him pronouns with me. My parents had been quiet. Dad nodded, just enough so that I knew he was listening. Mom was perfectly still. Like a statue. When I finished talking, there was this terrible, long silence. My brain filled each silent second with a hundred terrible ways this revelation could be a disaster. And that silence was . . . so long. Tens of thousands of terrible ways long.

"Sorry, honey, it's a lot to take in." That's what my mom said. I told her that I'm a boy, and the first thing she did was apologize. And I know she didn't mean for the words to hurt. I know she was just trying to understand.

But . . . it stung. It made me feel like there was something *I* needed to apologize for too.

Maybe Dad knew I was about to burst into tears because he swept in with a very simple question. Something to focus on for the next part of the conversation.

"So you want us to call you Linus?"

"Yes, please." I felt like I had to be polite. Like maybe if I got the request just right, they'd be able to magically get it. And it would stop being hard.

"And I'm guessing I know where the name came from, but would you like to tell us?"

"Oh, uh, sure." I looked uneasily at Mom, who had slow tears streaming down her cheeks. "I mean, uh, you named me after Grandma. So, uh, it made sense to me to, like, follow that tradition. So . . . I thought maybe using Grandpa's name would . . . keep in the spirit of my . . ." I froze then. The word *deadname* stuck in my throat.

"That's really thoughtful, Linus," Dad cut in.

"Finish what you were going to say, honey." I jumped at Mom's words. And her calling me *honey*. I'm sure she'd called me that before, but I didn't really remember. In that moment, it felt like a deliberate dig. Like she didn't want to say *Linus*. It made me sad. And kind of angry. But it also made it easier for me to say the next thing.

"Well, the term that people use for the name they

were given at birth is their deadname." I paused to look at my parents. They didn't react. Maybe this wasn't a new word for them. I went on. "I . . . that word . . . I mean, I didn't die. I just . . . understand myself a little better. So . . . I'm just calling it my old name." There was a long beat. *Just finish there. Don't do it. Don't say it*, my brain was nagging me . . . but I couldn't stop myself. "I hope that's okay."

It was Mom who responded that time. "Of course. Like your father said, sweetie, it's all very thoughtful. Not that that's a surprise. You're always . . . Well, you've always been a thoughtful kid." She drew me in for a hug, and I let her. When she pulled back, she smiled at me. I smiled back. I think. I don't really remember.

My parents messed up. A lot. In the beginning, they would say my old name and then fumble with some kind of apology. And each time my heart sputtered. Ached in a particular way.

So maybe what I'm feeling when Marigold looks over at me and waves enthusiastically isn't a sputter. Maybe it's more of a flutter.

Marigold seats herself next to someone who isn't me. I try not to be disappointed. But I am. My stomach does this weird droppy thing, and I can feel my ears getting hot, pushing heat into the sides of my face and through to my cheeks. Geez, I didn't even do anything embarrassing, and my body is still a mess.

Thankfully, Etta clomps into the room. Her green hair isn't as styled today. It looks like she just rolled out of bed, looked at the way her hair was poking out in nearly every direction, and decided to go with it. Which kind of works for her. I expect her to walk right past Mr. Todd, and I'm just about to raise my hand and wave her over to the empty seat next to me when she stops and slowly takes one of the nomination forms. Like, really slowly. Her expression is hard to read. Or maybe it looks like two things at once. On the one hand, she looks like she dares anyone to say anything about her taking the form. On the other hand, she looks sheepish, like maybe she knows this is something that she shouldn't be doing? Which is weird, 'cause Mr. Todd is practically *begging* students to take the nomination forms. He's probably like fifteen seconds away from offering extra credit.

I don't care how much extra credit Mr. Todd offers. I'm staying firmly out of the limelight and away from any microphones.

But Etta? Is Etta running for student council?

I try to check my reaction. I met Etta forty-eight hours ago. Maybe there are things I don't know about her yet. Shocking, right? Maybe she's got school spirit by the tons. Maybe she dyed her hair green because that's one of the school colors. Maybe she dresses up like the school mascot for home basketball games. What do I know?

When Etta turns to look at the room, I give her a wave and point to the empty seat next to me. Etta's face breaks out into a wide grin, and I almost forget that I was disappointed about Marigold sitting somewhere else. Now my heart is sighing—in a good way. It's nice to have a friend.

Mr. Todd is talking to someone else now, trying to convince them to take one of his forms.

"I got this for you," Etta says in a loud whisper as she flumps into the seat next to mine.

"Me?" I ask. I'm pretty sure my eyebrows aren't visible because they've risen so high that they're under my bushy hair.

"Yeah. You seem like . . ." She falters. "I think you'd be good at this."

"What's 'this' exactly?" I ask, crossing my arms. At first, I put them under my binder, but I am instantly worried that will make my boobs show up more than I want them to, so I readjust, crossing my arms just over my boobs. It feels weird. I'm sure it looks weird. But I stick with it. Because it would be weirder to cross my arms *two times* and then be like, "Oh, jk, I really just wanted to have my hands in my lap!"

Fortunately, Etta does not seem to notice that I am having a literal battle with my arms and my boobs. "Student council," she says with a nod. I get really still. Like the way a deer gets still when it hears a sound in the forest. Fight or flight. After a beat and no discernable reaction from me, Etta shrugs and looks away for a minute.

Mercifully, conversation ends as Mr. Todd starts class.

After a few minutes, Etta slides the nomination form toward me again. On the top, she's scrawled a note: *You could bring a fresh perspective because you're new to Doolittle!*

I blink. The exclamation point seems odd. Out of character. Almost as out of character as Etta going out for student council herself.

I pull out my mechanical pencil and draw a small question mark next to Etta's note.

"Just think about it," she whispers.

I don't want to say no outright, so I simply nod and pull the paper with the note on it under my civics book.

8
Etta

IT TURNS OUT I'M NOT THE ONLY ONE WHO ISN'T A "JOINER."

Even though Linus took the nomination form, I'm pretty sure it was just to get me to stop bugging him about student council. Which, unfortunately, is not going to work. Sorry, Linus, I'm going to have to push you. And I'm very stubborn. (Just ask my mom.)

I make a couple other attempts throughout the day. I comment to Linus as I walk him to English that it might be worth thinking about what his campaign platform might be (like I have any idea what a campaign platform is).

When we meet up for lunch, Linus says he's craving ice cream. I take the opening.

"You know . . . ," I say, "if you were on student council, you could probably get, like, an ice cream vending machine."

"Do those exist?" he asks, eyes wide.

Okay, not quite the response I was hoping for. But . . . it's something. "Uh, yeah," I say. "I saw one once. Like, at a rest stop maybe." I'm lying. But I have to keep this conversation going. Because I have to get Linus to run for student council. Because I have to defeat Marigold Stimpson.

"What did it look like? How did it work?"

Well, shoot. Now I have to come up with some fake details about an ice cream machine that doesn't exist. "Uh . . . I don't really remember." *Smooth move, ex-lax* (my mom's go-to phrase when she messes something up). *Way to kill the momentum!*

"Oh." Linus goes back to eating his sandwich, and I go back to my plate of pasta. Whenever I get pasta from the cafeteria, it usually means that they ran out of vegan ideas for me. I mean, pasta's okay. But it can get old. I slurp up a noodle and feel a drop of red sauce run down my chin.

"Well, what kind of ice cream would *we* want in the vending machine?" Linus asks.

"Huh?" I look up. Linus busts out laughing. "What?" I ask.

"Your chin! Your face!" he says, barely able to get the words out, he's laughing so hard.

I grin. "What? I'm a messy eater." I shrug. The nice thing about black clothes is that my messy eating rarely shows up to haunt me for the second half of the day.

Linus hands me a napkin, and I deliberately wipe everywhere *but* the spot on my chin. Linus giggles and points to the napkin. I look down. It's covered in red sauce. Like, I *thought* I only had that glob that I intentionally left on my chin, but it looks like my entire face was covered in the stuff. I laugh too, joining Linus. Then Linus, still shaking from laughter, lifts up his hand and makes our *funny* sign. I make it back at him as my laughter starts to calm down.

"I think it would be cool to have a Dippin' Dots machine," Linus says when we've got ourselves under control.

"That actually *would* be kind of cool," I say. And I mean it. "You can get ice cream lots of places, but Dippin' Dots are, like, a special treat."

"Yeah, and it might be kind of neat to have something special here," Linus says. "Like, sure, I don't really want to go to school this morning, but at least there's Dippin' Dots."

I smile at Linus in what I hope is an encouraging way. Do I think he can get the school to install a Dippin' Dots machine? Probably not. But maybe. And if this is the issue that gets Linus to consider putting his name on the ballot, I'm going to encourage the heck out of it.

We finish up lunch, chatting about ice cream flavors we particularly like—I mention that we should take a trip to Wilcox Dairy before they close for the season—and how the math homework was basically impossible—neither of us really wants to "show our work." When lunch ends, we have to split. Linus is going to orchestra, and I'm heading to the other end of the building for Spanish.

"The Dippin' Dots thing is such a good idea, Linus. I really think—"

"Look," Linus cuts me off. "Can you just lay off the student council thing? I don't really get what's going on with you wanting me to do it or whatever, but I just . . . I just want to be your friend without us talking about that every couple of minutes."

"Oh," I say. Shoot. This is a curveball. The corners of my mouth dip down. Not because I'm frowning. Well, I guess I'm frowning. But not on purpose. It's like my mouth has a mind of its own. "Of course. I just . . ." I almost say that I just thought he would be great at it, but I bite my tongue.

I'll have to figure out another way to get him interested.

———

I spend all of Spanish thinking about what my next step should be with Linus. I *should* be spending all of Spanish thinking about the terms related to the weather that are printed on the worksheet in front of me. At least that's what I should be doing according to Señor Levine. A point he makes abundantly clear when he asks me a question, and I answer with an over-the-top shrug and the words "No hablo español," with a terrible accent to boot. My comment derails the class for a solid five minutes and gets Señor Levine on a tirade about attention and respect for about five more. Honestly, I kind of tune out when he gets to the part about language study being an exercise in effort or whatever. I'm not really sure what he's trying to say. It doesn't matter. I've still got the Linus problem to deal with.

I don't have a good plan when the bell rings, and I pack up my stuff. I'm just about to walk out of the room when I hear Señor Levine say, "Etta, espera por favor." I think about bolting . . . I need a talking-to from a teacher like I need a trip to Camp Blood on Friday the 13th. But instead of following my flight instinct, I freeze and turn toward Señor Levine.

He deliberately goes to his board and shifts the arrow on his LANGUAGE IN USE magnet from Español to English.

"Etta, I want to talk about your answer today . . ." He sounds tired. Maybe he needs an after-lunch siesta.

"Yeah, sorry about that," I say, looking over my shoulder like I'm eager to get to math or something. To be clear, I'm absolutely not eager to get to math; I'm just ready to be done with this conversation.

"It just feels like you weren't even attending to the lesson."

I blink. Then I cross my arms and say the most shocking thing I can think of. "I wasn't."

Señor Levine tilts his head. He doesn't look shocked per se, but at least he's stopped talking.

But then I say something that shocks me. "I'm distracted because I'm trying to make a new friend, and I'm worried I'm messing it up."

DANGER! DANGER! Where the heck did that come from?!

"Oh, well. That can be hard," Señor Levine says, his voice stilted.

"So, yeah. I wasn't really paying attention." I don't say I'll do better. Because I probably won't. And while I might be a little on the misanthropic side, I generally try not to be an outright liar.

"For what it's worth, I think the answer to your attention issue in Spanish and your issue with your friend might be basically the same."

"And what's that?" I say, sinking into my hip and pulling my arms tighter across my chest.

"Just be present in the moment. Attend to what's in front of you."

"Okay," I say, and turn to leave. "Whatever," I mutter under my breath.

━━━

Shockingly, I spend the next twenty-four hours actually trying to follow Señor Levine's advice. I shove the bet with Marigold out of my head as best I can and focus on actually talking to Linus.

In math class, I learn that Linus can't resist making puns. Even if they're a stretch. He drew a crude picture of a "Mathemachicken" on the side of his notes. It was hard to look at. And hilarious.

While at school we mostly crack jokes, when we're texting after school, Linus tells me how he misses his best friend from home, Olive. She sounds pretty cool, honestly.

> **Linus:** Yeah
>
> **Linus:** She's great
>
> **Me:** Be careful. Your new friend might get jealous.
>
> **Linus:** I can have more than one friend
>
> **Me:** I've only ever managed to have one at a time.
>
> **Me:** Sometimes zero.

I hit send on the texts in quick succession. It's like my fingers have a mind of their own. I want to call the words back. Scrub them out of being. This is too personal. Too—

> **Linus:** That sounds hard
>
> **Me:** Yeah.
>
> **Linus:** You don't have to talk about it if you don't
> want to

I type a few random paragraphs about Marigold. I don't use her name of course, but I talk about our friendship. And how it ended in a way I still don't understand.

> **Linus:** Sorry
> **Linus:** That's the pits
> **Linus:** 🍎
> **Linus:** I a-peach-iate you
> **Linus:** Get it?

I laugh. I was in the middle of feeling sad and sorry, and Linus manages to make me laugh. What a good guy.

I send him a video of me doing the *that's funny* gesture.

Linus sends one back.

9

Linus

**WHEN A NEW FRIEND INVITES YOU OVER, YOU SAY YES!
EVEN IF YOU DON'T WANT TO WATCH HORROR MOVIES! AND
PARTICULARLY IF IT GETS YOU OUT OF FAMILY DINNER WITH
YOUR GRANDMOTHER!**

I'm making a friendship bracelet for Etta when Mom comes to my room to talk about tomorrow's dinner.

"Hey, Liney," she says softly as she knocks on the door.

"Hey." I look over at the mess I've made. Finding my embroidery floss meant rooting through my closet and pulling out my unpacked boxes from the move until I found one labeled: L BEDROOM: CRAFTS. The box was filled with origami paper, sewing supplies, and a truly obscene number of cootie catchers, which I scattered all over the floor in pursuit of my plastic embroidery floss box and the clipboard I use to hold the end of the strings steady.

"Any homework?"

"Mountains," I respond, holding up the half-made bracelet. She crosses her arms, saying *I'm serious* without saying anything. "It's the first week of school, Mom. It's all getting to know you and fluff," I lie. I do have homework. In math. I mean, I did it already, and it didn't go well. But mentioning my math skills aren't quite up to snuff at my new school seems like an invitation for more conversations with my mother.

I'm honestly expecting Mom to see that I'm occupied and move on, but she doesn't. She comes into the room and starts putting the crafts I'm not using back in the box.

"I didn't know you kept this stuff," she says absently.

"Why wouldn't I keep it?" I ask.

"I dunno. I just didn't know you were still into this."

I tense. Because I'm not quite sure if she means she wonders because I shifted my interests or if it's because I'm a boy and I *shouldn't* like crafting or something.

"Nope, I still make friendship bracelets," I say. I push some extra chipper-ness into my tone. "This one is for my new friend Etta."

"Oh, that's great! It's so good that you're already making friends, Liney."

I nod. I'm glad about making friends too. But part of me is still tense.

"I think we're going to go to a restaurant with your grandma tomorrow night," Mom says. I don't respond, just keep knotting the threads in the bracelet. I picked dark green colors and alternate them with black so there

is a faint stripe pattern. The combination feels like Etta.
"Remember, I mentioned we would be doing family dinners twice a week?" Mom goes on. I guess not responding
wasn't the right answer.

"Yeah. I remember."

"So, is there any food you want to try? We could look
for a Chinese spot here or maybe find some Thai?"

"Thai could be good," I say, trying to brighten my
voice, feigning some enthusiasm.

I'm just not looking forward to spending more time
with Grandma. Because I'm not really sure what to say
to her when she messes up my name or pronouns. And
thinking about having to say something in the first place
just makes me mad. I don't like feeling mad. Better to just
avoid thinking about it.

"Okay, I'll look it up. And chat with Grandma about
it. I just figured we could only handle so many Mickey
waffles for dinner."

The Mickey waffles are the least of my worries when
it comes to dinner with Grandma.

✕

I spend most of Friday dreading dinner. Etta isn't at
school in the morning, which means I can't give her the
friendship bracelet, so it just sits in my bag and makes
me wonder if I'm weird for deciding to make it for her.

So I guess most of my thinking time is spent worrying about dinner and wondering what Etta will think of the bracelet. On the way back to my locker from orchestra, I pop into the bathroom, go straight into a stall—thank goodness there's an open one—and whip out my phone.

There's a message from Mom.

> **Mom:** I hope school is going great! Found a Thai place!

I navigate away without responding and scroll over to my conversation with Etta. I texted her at lunch to see if she was okay, but she hasn't responded yet. Maybe she's sick and resting. I don't want to disturb her. So I move over to my thread with Olive. I take a deep breath and start typing. I need a break from thinking about dinner.

> **Me:** Remember what you said about running for student council?

Okaaaaay, that isn't quite what I thought I wanted to talk about. But Olive responds almost immediately.

> **Olive:** 👀👀👀
>
> **Me:** Don't get too excited
>
> **Olive:** 2 late

Me: It's just weird.

Me: Cause you made that joke

Me: And now I have a friend here who's talking to me about it

Olive: Awww! You made a friend!

Olive: DONT REPLACE ME!!!!!!! 😫😫

I do a half chuckle–half sigh and think, *Oh, Olive!* in my head. Olive never holds back in talking about what she thinks. *She* probably would have said something to my parents if she'd been there at dinner with my grandma.

Me: Of course

Me: Also not talking about that right now

Olive: oh right

Olive: SC

SC? Oh, that must mean *student council.* I sit still as the three dots show up on my screen. I'm not saying I'll base my next steps on what Olive says. But I'm not *not* saying that. Sometimes it's easier to take the decision-making out of my own hands. Then I don't overthink so much.

Olive: i say go for it

Olive: something to do!

Olive: ok . . . need to go back to class

I take another breath and slide my phone into my pocket. First Marigold with her texts, then Etta, now Olive. Maybe I *should* be thinking about student council? I mean, I never really thought of it as my thing. But when I was little, I didn't think being a boy was really my thing. And . . . here we are. Maybe I should give it a try?

What's the worst that happens?

Well, that was the absolute wrong question to ask because now my brain is spinning with roughly 523 worst-case scenarios. Which isn't good.

At least I'm not thinking about my grandmother.

Oh, wait. Now I am. Shoot.

When I get to math, I slide into an open desk. My leg immediately starts bouncing, up-and-down-and-up-and-down. I normally would worry that other kids can hear a tiny thumping sound, but I'm too amped up thinking about student council.

Etta is still absent in math, so there's a spot open next to me because no one really knows me other than Etta and Marigold, kind-of. And Marigold isn't in this class. I wish I didn't know all the classes we share by heart—civics, English, and gym—but I do. Etta and I only have civics and math together. But those are my first and last classes of the day, so at least we get to start and end the day together. Except not today. Because she isn't here.

But then, she is. She walks through the doorway like a breath of fresh air dressed in a doom-and-gloom costume. I sit up straighter and wave her over. She almost skips when she sees me and sits down next to me.

"Are you okay?" I ask.

"Yeah, fine. I overslept. And my mom . . . let me. She says that if my body needs sleep, I need to give it sleep." She rolls her eyes, but there's a wry smile on her lips. Her faded black lipstick frames her teeth.

I think about giving Etta the friendship bracelet, but midway through math class doesn't really seem like the right time. Maybe after school.

Class goes by without a mention of student council, even though I'm ready for Etta to bring it up again. And ready to tell her that I think I'm going to do it. I'm eager to see her reaction. Instead, we do our best to correct our abysmal attempts at the homework and crack quiet jokes to each other every so often. I feel this odd sense of relief when I see that Etta isn't totally on top of polynomials either. Last night, when I was struggling through the assignment, I worried that maybe my school in New York had just taught me totally different stuff. Or wrong stuff. But seeing that it seems to make just as much—or little—sense to Etta calms me down. Surely if other kids are struggling too, the teacher will help?

I startle when Mx. B, the math teacher, comes up to my desk and crouches down next to me.

"Hi, Linus," Mx. B says in a hushed voice. "We've had

about a week together, but I wanted to check in, since you're new to Doolittle and are coming with a different math background."

"Um, thanks," I say. I opt not to go into the details of my *math background*. All I really know is that it wasn't this.

"Could you do me a favor and do your corrections on a separate sheet of paper?" Mx. B asks. They're nonbinary and use they/them pronouns, which is the first time I've encountered an adult who does that. Even though Mx. B doesn't know I'm trans, it makes me feel a little less alone. But then I look around the room and notice that no one else is doing their work on a separate sheet of paper.

Lonely, party of one.

"Why?" I ask. I try to sound curious and not rude or unreasonable.

"I just want to get to know you as a mathematician. We learn just as much from our missteps as we do our successes. If I can see all your work clearly, I'll be able to help you bridge some of the inevitable gaps that come with switching schools."

I nod. It's . . . a very nice explanation. It doesn't particularly make me feel better about having to do something different than everyone else, but at least they seem to have good intentions.

"And Linus . . . it's only the first week. We'll get you where you need to go."

I'm not really sure what Mx. B means by that, but I nod and give them an I-totally-get-it smile.

I spend the next twenty minutes working on corrections that I'm not quite sure are fixing anything. Then we move on to the lesson. I try to focus, but with the end of the day looming, dinner with Grandma is back to consume all my thoughts.

When the bell rings, I'm half stressed mess / half zombie-walking-to-my-doom.

As we make our way to our lockers, Etta asks, "What's your favorite horror movie?"

"What?" I ask.

"What's your favorite horror movie?"

"Uh . . . I don't really watch horror movies."

"Like, at all?" Etta sounds, well, *horrified*. Haha!

"Aren't I too young or something?" I open my eyes wide. The picture of innocence.

Etta puts her hand on my shoulder and makes a big show of stopping us both in our tracks so she can bring her hand up and wiggle it. The *that's funny* gesture. She might not laugh, but she seems to get my humor. But then she stops and slams her hands to her sides. Maybe this is, like, another version of the *anti-funny* sign? We seem to be coming up with a lot of those.

"No, seriously," she says.

I shrug. What can I say?

"Are you telling me you are seriously thirteen years old and you haven't seen a single horror movie? Not even, like, *Halloween* or *Friday the 13th* or *A Nightmare on Elm Street*?"

"Is that the one with . . . Jack?" I know it isn't.

Etta gives me a deadpan look. Like she's about to make her very own horror movie right here, right now. And I'm going to be the first casualty.

"Jack . . . O'-Lantern?" I squeak. Finishing the joke at my own peril.

"Linuuuuuuus." She drags out the *U* sound in a whiny, horrified way.

"Not funny?"

"No. This is serious. Linus." I like all the different ways she comes up with to say my name.

And maybe because I'm enjoying poking this particular bear, I ask, "Does *Hocus Pocus* count?"

"Does—Does?—*Hocus Poc*—? LINUS!" She grabs my hand and drags me down the hall toward the school exit.

"I don't have any of my—"

"Linus, do you think your English homework matters at a time like this?!" She's dragging me along, but I'm definitely going along with the drag.

Once we get outside, Etta shields her eyes and looks down the line of cars waiting to pick up kids.

"Who's picking you up?" she asks. "What do they drive?"

"Uh, my mom, and she drives a silver SUV."

Etta gives me a look that says that my description is unhelpful. There's a sea of SUVs in the school's driveway. And half of them are silver.

"There's a cactus on the antenna that, like, dances when we drive."

"Geez, Linus. Of course there is." She rolls her eyes. "You couldn't have led with that?"

As it turns out, Mom's is the second car in line, which is both nice and embarrassing. Nice because, well, my mom is here. Embarrassing because how long has she been here to get this primo spot in the line?

Etta starts waving frantically at Mom, who rolls the window down.

"Hi, Linus's mom!" Etta trills in a voice I've never heard her use before. It's completely at odds with her usual emo-almost-punk, all-black look. It's approachable, friendly. I mean, Etta *is* those things, but it doesn't seem like she wants people to know she is. "I'm Etta! Linus and I met at school!"

"Nice to meet you, Etta." I silently thank Mom for just being normal. Even though Etta is very definitely left of normal.

"Well, I was wondering . . . Linus is new to school

and all, and it would be great if we could, you know, hang out? Would that be okay? We can call my mom so you can do that mom thing where you size each other up."

"Yeah, and make sure she's not a serial killer," I chip in. Etta jabs me with her elbow, and my mom gives me one of those don't-be-weird-in-front-of-company looks. Which makes me laugh because I was just thinking the same thing at her.

"Sure, Etta, let's give your mother a call. What's her number?"

"Here, I'll call her and let her talk to you. That way the call won't be screened."

Etta's performance continues as she animatedly talks to her mom and then hands the phone over to my mom, who asks all the required mom questions and says that she'll text so Etta's mom has her number and that she plans to pick me up after dinner and, oh yes, it *would* be great if the kids could do homework together.

After Etta recites her mom's number so my mom can add it to her phone, Mom says goodbye and tacks on a "We'll talk when you get home, Liney." I nod, but I don't have time to stress because Etta is dragging me back into the building. Honestly, I don't *need* to stress. I get to hang out with Etta, and I don't have to have dinner with Grandma anymore. I'm just relieved.

"Wait, why are we going back?" I ask.

"Because I know you were about to freak out about not having all your stuff, Linus." Etta says it like she's annoyed, but I can tell that she's secretly being really, really thoughtful. I smile at her. And she rolls her eyes.

10
Etta

THERE'S NOTHING LIKE A GOOD HORROR MOVIE. AND THIS IS NOTHING LIKE A GOOD HORROR MOVIE. BUT IT DOESN'T SUCK. (DON'T TELL ANYONE I SAID THAT LAST PART.)

We don't end up watching a horror movie. In part because I'm having a hard time nailing down which one is just right for starting Linus on his journey to becoming a horror movie aficionado and in part because I can tell that Linus is, like, actually terrified (and I don't want to scare away my new friend and ticket to revenge against Marigold Stimpson).

We *do* watch *Hocus Pocus*. I use the word *watch* loosely because we talk through the whole thing. Very occasionally we remark on the movie (Mary Sanderson is an icon) and more often we chat about Linus's old school in New York or the farm camp I went to in Amish Country when I was in fifth grade or about how Linus has no siblings and I have one—a very annoying older brother. It's pretty easy to talk to Linus.

I don't bring up student council.

Honestly, I don't even think about it while we're hanging out. Linus just engages. He always seems interested in what I have to say. And I'm interested in what he has to say. It's . . . weird. Or, I mean, I haven't had another person like this. Not since Marigold. I shove down the unpleasant feeling that's crawling up my throat. Gross.

"So, there are a couple of things I want to say," Linus announces as the credits for *Hocus Pocus* roll across the screen. It's a real change in tone. He suddenly feels very formal. "Uh . . ." He scuttles off the bed and gets something out of his backpack. "I was thinking about what you shared yesterday, and I made you this." He sheepishly opens his hand. Inside, there's a twisted mass of black-and-green thread. And then I realize what I'm looking at. It's a friendship bracelet.

"Sorry if this is too forward or weird, but it just felt like the right thing to do." Linus's eyes get round as he waits for me to do something.

I reach over and pluck the bracelet from his hand. It's a simple design, probably eight threads, just repeating over and over in rows of knots. Marigold made Vs and fish in hers, but this one seems better to me. More fitting.

"Thanks," I say, wrapping it around my wrist instantly. I don't know that I can say much more because, to my horror, I almost feel like crying. The way the bracelet slides against my wrist is both familiar and completely new at the same time. I didn't know I missed the feeling of a friendship bracelet.

"I mean, it's okay if you just want to—"

I interrupt and hold my wrist out to him. "Can you tie it on?" I ask.

He does. As his fingers tie the threads, he says, "About student council . . ."

"What now?" I ask, shocked that Linus is the one bringing this up. I get very still, like I might spook him if I make any sudden movements.

"I've just . . . I've been thinking about student council. And maybe . . ."

Maybe?! Maybe what? My eyes widen.

"Maybe we could look into it. If, um, *you'd* be willing to help me. Because I'm still new. I don't know what I don't know, you know?"

"Sure." My voice is almost a whisper. I can't believe it! I got exactly what I wanted, and I didn't have to *do* anything. Linus gives me a tentative smile, so I give him one back. "What made you change your mind?"

Linus gives me a pensive look. "It wasn't one thing exactly. It just . . . The universe kept putting the idea out there. You and, well, some of my other friends brought it up." Other friends? Who are Linus's other friends? The only person I've seen him talk to at school is Marigold. Did she actually convince him to do this? Is she toying with him? To toy with me?!

Wow. I'm, like, *super* territorial, huh?

"Anyway, it just seems like, I dunno, it's something to try." Linus runs his hand through his hair and gives me a tentative smile.

"For sure," I say.

"But can you tell me, for real? Why did you keep bringing it up?"

Linus is really the king of curveballs. I didn't expect this. For a moment I think about telling him. About Marigold. About our broken friendship. About Nova. About how I need to get into that school more than I need air. And about just . . . needing to be right. For once.

But I don't.

Instead, I say another truth.

"I . . . Honestly, I just think school would be better if I knew that people like you were . . . looking after things."

It's not the real truth. Not the exact reality. But that doesn't make it a lie.

Linus's mom picks him up after dinner.

"We'll do horror movies next time," I say. Linus goes pale, so I add, "We'll work you up. Won't start with anything too gory."

"I hope you're keeping things PG-13," Linus's mom says. She gives my mom a worried look, but she doesn't seem to notice.

"Oh, yeah. Sure," I agree. I mean, I have every intention of traumatizing her son, but I'm not gonna tell her to her face! When they walk away, Linus looks back at me and I mouth, "No," and make a slashing motion across my throat. He looks worried, but then he smiles and puts his hand out in front of him and wiggles it.

I wave at Linus as his mom pulls out of the driveway. When I turn back, touching the friendship bracelet with the tips of my fingers, Mom is waiting.

"He seems nice," she says, smiling.

"He *is* nice." I scoff. I roll my eyes as I push past her, but it's a half-hearted roll at best. Linus is nice. He's probably the nicest person I've ever met. And, for some reason, he wants to be my friend.

"What's on deck for homework, Etta? It didn't look like you got much done with your friend."

"Math. Eternally," I respond.

"Anything else?"

"Uh, yeah, now that you mention it. Linus is going to run for student council and I'm gonna be, like, his campaign manager?"

Mom looks genuinely surprised. "Really?"

"You don't have to act so shocked," I say, annoyance in my voice.

"Excuse me for calling them like I see them." Mom turns to the kitchen table to finish clearing the remnants of dinner. She opted to order pizza when she realized there wasn't something more than PB&J to offer company. She got one small vegan pizza for me and a large pepperoni pizza for everyone else—which included Linus, Jamie (who ate three pieces in a single bite and ran out of the house to work), and her.

I think about Marigold's taunt at the assembly. About how she called me *anti-everything*.

I tentatively walk over to the sink and start to rinse off the plates Mom has piled up on the counter.

"Oh, you don't need to worry about that, Etta. I know you have eternal math."

I know she's making a joke, but I don't have a sympathy laugh in me. I just slowly move the plates under the hypnotic stream of water and watch flecks of cheese and blobs of sauce slide off.

I'm finishing up the last plate when I say, "Do you think that I . . . I dunno . . . that I'm anti-everything?"

Mom stops moving and comes to stand next to me. She seems to know that I don't want to look at her head-on. Instead, she moves the cups closer to me so I can reach and rinse them.

"What do you mean by that, Etta?"

"I know I dress a certain way. But . . . do you think that means I don't care about anything?"

"Oh, Bubby . . . ," Mom says. That's her nickname for me. Bubby. Not that she's used it much lately. She didn't know if I was going to be a girl or a boy when she was pregnant, so she made up all these nicknames. That's the one that stuck. "I think sometimes people make assumptions based on what we look like."

I nod and keep filling the dishwasher. Cup. Cup. Fork. Knife. The fork and the knife were used by Mom. Linus was horrified. He mouthed, "Your mom is a MONSTER," and I cracked up. Linus looked absolutely delighted that he had managed to get a genuine giggle out of me.

"And sometimes, a lot of eyeliner, green hair, and all-black clothes can make people think . . . I don't know. That you won't care what people think. But . . . you obviously care. No one forces their mother to spend their entire Sunday before the start of school meticulously dyeing their hair because they don't care."

I laugh, remembering that just last Sunday, I'd wanted to make a statement for the first day of school. Even if the statement was STAY AWAY.

"So, no. I don't think you're anti-everything. You're anti–animal cruelty and anti-racist and anti-homework, but anti-everything? No way."

She gives me a sideways hug because I'm still refusing to look at her. Out of principle. Mom can say nice things all she wants, but that doesn't mean I have to look at her while she's doing it.

"Anyway, I'm helping Linus run for student council. I mean, it probably won't work, but—"

"Why do you say that?" Mom asks.

"Things just don't seem to work out for me." I shrug. I know Mom is about 0.7 seconds away from saying, "Like what?" so instead of facing *that*, I say, "Homework beckons," and run up the stairs two at a time.

In my room, I pull up my favorite horror movie of late: *Carrie*. A classic that would definitely not be approved by Linus's mother. Especially when one of the first things on the screen is a shower scene full of boobs and Carrie getting her first period and losing it. To be honest, it's just as well Linus isn't watching this one with me. He wouldn't know what to do with the period blood and tampon throwing.

I keep watching. Man, the teachers at this school suck. They slap Carrie and mess up her name even when she corrects them. I mean, I know it's an old movie, but did teachers really used to act this way? Ugh! I would have developed telekinesis too! Or at least a whole lot of trauma . . .

I let the movie run in the background as I pull up the Nova website and click through the reminder about the open house next Sunday. Then I navigate to the application. *Name. Birthday. Parent name.* Okay . . . this seems doable. I scroll through to the essay questions. *What qualities make you uniquely suited to contribute to the Nova community?* I sigh as I stare at the question and the seemingly huge text box beneath it. I don't know. Do they need someone sarcastic? Someone who is over middle school? Someone who knows horror movies inside and out? Are those qualities that make me uniquely suited to do whatever it is they are looking for?

I slam my laptop closed and grab my math homework. It's a dark day when math homework is the lesser of two evils.

I pull out my phone and text Linus. At least talking to him about math homework (and whatever else we want to talk about) makes it bearable.

Me: lmk when u start math
Me: won't get far without you . . .

Linus doesn't answer right away. I try not to read into that. He's probably still in the car with his mom. Or updating his dad about the week at school. Even though there are all kinds of reasons he can't respond, I keep checking my phone.

11

Linus

JUST TRYING TO GET THROUGH THE DAY UNSCATHED!
AND FAILING!

"So, dinner with your grandmother was nice. We ended up going to an Italian place. We wanted to save the Thai spot for you," Mom says as we drive back home. I didn't realize it before, but Etta's house is pretty close to mine. Less than ten blocks away.

"Okay. Thanks," I mutter.

"Grandma asked about you," Mom prods.

I stop myself from saying the words that fly into my mind. From asking if she managed to remember that I'm Linus and a boy.

"You know, there might not be many dinners like this left when Grandma is healthy," Mom adds.

"Really, because it seems like we're planning a million of them!" Whoops. That slipped out.

"Linus!" Mom sounds shocked as she pulls into the driveway. As soon as the car stops, I open my door and go into the house.

I run to my room, something like shame crawling up from my spine and warming my cheeks. I can't believe I talked back to my mom. And it felt awful. I thought that saying what I was thinking would feel freeing? Like I would finally feel like myself. But my comment clangs around in my head—ugly and horrible. And true.

It isn't Mom who knocks on my bedroom door a few minutes later. It's Dad.

I roll over and put my back to him. A mix of anger and shame keep me staring at the wall. I hear Dad's heavy footsteps as he moves into the room and comes toward the bed, which slumps when he sits on it.

"So, I think your mom talked to you a bit in the car. Right, tiger?"

I don't say anything.

"Any thoughts?"

I wait. A part of me hopes that if I don't say anything for long enough, he'll just give up and walk away. And another part of me is soothed that he's here and willing to talk to me, even though I did something rude.

Finally, after I've given Dad enough of an opportunity to give up on me, I roll over and look at him. I wonder what would happen if I told him. Not if I burst out with a snarky comment, but if I told him that dinner with Grandma on Monday made me uncomfortable and the thought of future dinners doesn't sound so great either.

"Are you mad?" I finally say, testing the waters.

"Me? No." Dad says the words simply. Like they're easy to say. Maybe that means he really *isn't* mad.

"But I said something rude."

"You're a kid. A *teen* at that," he says with a shrug. "It's part of the territory."

I sit up. "Oh, yeah. Hormone changes and big feelings and all that . . ."

"Exactly."

I decide to try to talk to Dad. "I kind of meant it though," I say.

"Meant what?"

"What I said about having so many dinners with Grandma. It feels like that's all we do anymore. Just . . . have dinner with Grandma and talk about having dinner with Grandma."

"Oh. Well, that's a fair point. We're still figuring out the routine though." Dad tilts his head a bit, like he's thinking.

"And . . ." I'm going to do it. I'm going to share what's really bothering me. I take a breath and look down at the floor. "It makes me uncomfortable when she uses the wrong pronouns for me."

"Oh." Dad's voice is quieter now. "Yeah, that probably doesn't feel so good." He pauses for a second and then says, "Did you know when I started dating your mother, your grandmother called me Jim for a solid two months? I think that was your mom's old boyfriend or something. I thought it meant that she didn't think I would stick around long enough to make learning my name worth it." He chuckles.

I don't laugh. It isn't funny to me.

"But she got there. I'm Doug now."

"And I'm Linus," I say.

"Yep. You are." He claps his hand on my shoulder and pulls me in for a hug. I hug him back. It's a hollow hug though. I can't quite get my arms to squeeze the way they normally do. The conversation wasn't exactly bad, but it didn't do what I hoped. Even though I know I was the one who said something rude in the first place, I still thought that maybe after Dad came up to see me, he would make me feel better. Instead, he basically told me to wait it out. We'll see though. Maybe he's right. Maybe the next dinner will be better.

"I have a great idea," Etta proclaims when I pick up a call from her on Sunday morning. I've spent most of the weekend sleeping. Or at least not vertical. I guess going to a new school takes a lot of energy.

"Let's hear it," I say. Despite it being the weekend, I'm tired. And I sound over whatever it is she's going to suggest already. I'm not over it. I'm really eager to hear whatever Etta wants to suggest. I'm just worn down, I guess.

"Well, there's no school tomorrow because it's Labor Day, and we need to spend some time together getting ready for the student council Q&A this coming week, right?" Etta's voice sounds way perkier than normal as she says the words. I wait for whatever she's going to suggest. "And I love horror movies and Halloween-y stuff."

"Okay . . . ," I say.

"And you probably love going to petting farms, right?"

"I mean, that sounds better than, like, watching horror movies, I guess."

"Exactly! Well, there's this farm just past the Michigan border, about thirty minutes away. It has a petting farm. Aaaaand . . . it also has a haunted barn that opens this weekend!" She pauses, no doubt waiting for me to respond. To love this idea as much as she does. "Something for you. Something for me. And a long car ride there and back to talk about how to best present yourself to the eighth grade on Wednesday at assembly."

"Um . . ." *Come on, Linus. Muster up some enthusiasm. This is new friend Etta talking! It's not like you're booked and dodging invitations to house parties and sleepovers. Just say something! Anything!*

But it's Etta who talks next, offering some more persuasion. "Come on. It's just a silly haunted barn. It's not, like, actually scary at all. Plus, we can go before it even gets dark."

Okay. That's pretty thoughtful actually. And maybe it's like the *Hocus Pocus* of haunted houses? More campy and entertaining than truly terrifying. Besides, Etta seems really into it.

"Yeah, sure. Let me talk to my parents about it. When are you thinking?"

"My mom and I can come and pick you up around four."

It's Sunday, so I'm not missing another dinner with Grandma. That's tomorrow.

"My mom could call your mom to talk about it if you want," Etta suggests. Her enthusiasm is flagging a bit. Maybe she's sensing my anxiety. "Moms have a harder time saying no to other moms."

"That might be good," I concede.

"Great!" Etta says. "I'll have her call your mom, and then we get to kick off spooky season together!"

"Spooky season? It's September."

"Yeah . . . and that's honestly kinda on the late side for me to be getting going on all this. Usually, I have my Halloween costume planned in August."

"August? What if you change your mind?"

"Great art takes time! And trust me, my Halloween costumes are art."

"Well, I'm looking forward to seeing what you do this year."

"Oh, maybe we'll do a tandem costume!" Etta exclaims.

I blush. Etta thinks of me not only as her new friend but, maybe, as her Halloween costume buddy. That's . . . that's real. That's not just being nice—though it's not like Etta is ever *just* being nice. It's something solid. Something true.

12

Etta

IS THIS MY GREATEST IDEA TO DATE? PROBABLY.

Linus is all business on the ride up to Michigan. He's got a fresh notebook and a purple pen, and he's eager to write down everything we talk about in mind-numbing detail. It's nice that he cares about this, I guess. Makes my job to turn him into a winner that much easier.

"Okay," I say, "let's start by thinking of all the qualities that would make you good at this."

Linus turns pink.

"I can list things, and you can just write them down, if you want," I offer. Linus nods and pulls the cap off his pen.

"Well, for starters, you have a good sense of humor." When Linus doesn't move to start his list of good qualities, I make a scribbling gesture with my hand. "Add it to the list, dude."

"I have a good sense of humor? Says who?"

"Your constant need to make jokes," I shoot back.

"Making jokes isn't the same as having a good sense

of humor. Particularly if you're the only one laughing." Linus thinks for a second and then says, "Double particularly if you're laughing *at* someone and inviting others to do the same. Which I don't do. But I just felt it needed to be said."

"Well, there's another thing. You care about other people."

"Doesn't everybody?" he asks.

"First of all. No." A stray thought passes through my mind that *I* don't particularly care about *anyone.* "Second of all. *Linus!* The point of this list is just to come up with as many ideas as possible, not to . . . shoot down everything that doesn't make you . . ." I can't quite think of the right words, but the question from the Nova application comes flying into my mind. ". . . uniquely suited to contribute to the community as a member of the student council."

"Fine." Linus still doesn't move to write anything, so I snatch the notebook from his hands.

"I'll write it myself." I hold out my hand, demanding the pen.

Linus sighs and hands it over, grumbling about how it'll probably be better this way anyway.

"And I'm adding the thing about a good sense of humor." I say the words like they're a threat. The list is in my hands now. I'm in charge. I'll write down all the nice things about Linus that I want!

"I think we need some empirical evidence. You giving

me a pity hand gesture whenever I crack a dad joke isn't the same as . . . making anyone else laugh or happy."

"Linus!" I'm starting to get frustrated. "What about your T-shirt collection?" I look at today's tee: a *Star Wars*–themed shirt for the Kessel Fun-Run (which is billed as being twelve parsecs long—a super-deep pull for *Star Wars* fans).

"What if my mom buys all my shirts?" Linus hedges. "Oh, I know! Put that my mom has a sense of humor on the list!"

He seems genuinely excited about this idea, which is . . . weird. But I laugh a little and just let him go. We keep brainstorming from there. Linus tries to hold back his natural desire to fight me on every nice thing I have to say about him. We add:

FRESH PERSPECTIVE ABOUT DOOLITTLE
EASY TO TALK TO
GOOD SMILE
GOOD HEART

The sky is a brilliant pink and orange when we pull into the parking lot for Dover's Haunted Barn and Petting Farm.

"On the way back, we'll talk strategy," I say, opening the car door and hopping out.

"Strategy?" Linus asks as he places the paper and pen

in his backpack, unbuckles his seat belt, and trundles out of the car with his entire backpack in tow.

"Sure. I mean, you're a strong candidate." The words feel foreign in my mouth. Out of place. I try to push past it, to make it sound like I know what I'm talking about. "But, like, you still have to beat other people. So we'll talk about how to do that."

"Do you know how to do that?" Linus asks, his eyes round.

"I mean . . . I think we can both agree that between the two of us, I have the killer instinct."

"But you're not going to, uh, do anything to anyone?"

"You mean start a smear campaign?" I ask. The idea sounds kind of fun. Particularly if it were a smear campaign against Marigold.

Linus must see that I'm considering the idea because his eyes get huge. "No!" he almost shouts. "Turn away from the dark side, Etta!"

I bust out laughing. I know that Linus is serious in his demand that his campaign not go negative, but he also is kind of funny.

"Okay! Okay!" I finally concede through my laughter. "But *you* have to agree that 'good sense of humor' belongs on the list."

"Fine," Linus grumbles, clutching his backpack to his chest. "But I'm keeping the thing about my mom on there too."

"You don't want to leave that in the car?" I ask, pointing to the backpack.

"No. I—" He stops talking suddenly and blushes. Or maybe it's just the pink of the sky reflecting off his cheeks. "What if inspiration hits? Maybe I need to run a haunted barn–themed campaign?"

"Or a llama-themed one!" I say, pointing to a llama silhouetted in the barn door.

"That feels more like me. I'll start spelling my name with two Ls. It'll be a whole thing."

"Double-L-Linus. Very cerebral," I say solemnly. Trying hard not to crack up.

"I'm gonna run and grab a kid-free coffee," Mom says. "You guys have fun. Keep in text-touch. What do you think . . . like two hours until pickup?" I give her a nod and grab Linus by the wrist.

"What should we do first?"

Linus looks nervously in the direction of the haunted barn. It has a sign over the door with the letters painted in a cheesy font to look like blood. It really isn't scary. Like, at all.

But apparently, it looks scary to Linus. Because he isn't really moving.

"You wanna start slow, Double-L-Linus?" I ask.

Linus nods, and I tug him toward the petting farm.

13
Linus

I GUESS I HAVE TO FACE THE FACT THAT I AM TERRIFIED OF A FAKE HAUNTED BARN.

It takes about seven minutes to wrap up our grand tour of the petting farm. We saw the llama—of course—a horse, four pigs, six chickens, and three goats. We tried to extend our stay by feeding the animals, but the food pellet dispensers were all empty.

As we walk through the farm, I can hear the occasional screams of people who braved the haunted barn. My brain is a war zone. On the one hand, I really-really-really-like-beyond-100-percent do NOT want to go in that haunted barn. I don't care how silly it is. On the other hand, I don't want to let Etta down.

"Okay. Time to be brave and face down the zombie farmers or whatever else we might find in the haunted barn." Etta says *haunted barn* a little bit like Dracula and raises her hands and wiggles her fingers like she's casting some sort of spell. Or curse.

A cramp snakes through my belly.

"Uh, I have to go to the bathroom," I say. I take a sharp left turn toward a row of porta-potties bordering a dried-out cornfield. I keep my eyes on the rows of corn, half expecting some guy with a plaid shirt and a chain-saw to jump out and scare me. Etta follows. I turn back to her and say, "You . . . you go ahead."

"What? No way! We came here together. Besides, my mom says I should never miss an opportunity to use the bathroom!"

I sigh and let Etta follow me to the porta-potties.

In the safety of the bathroom, I linger longer than I should, hoping that I'll be able to come up with some reasonable way to get Etta to go into the haunted barn without me.

My phone buzzes in my pocket. It's Mom.

Mom: Hope you are having fun with your friend! Send me proof of life.

Mom: We ended up taking Grandma to the movies!

Then a picture of Grandma sitting in a movie theater seat with a massive bucket of popcorn in her lap comes through. I sigh, relieved that I missed another evening of grandmother-focused time.

When we first moved to Ohio, my mom sat me down to have a big talk about why we moved here. The main reason, according to her, was to spend time with my grandmother. And one way we were going to do that was by having regular dinners with her.

I really, really, really wanted to say "That's why you *dragged* me away from my home and my best friend. That is not why *I* moved here."

It's not that I don't like my grandmother. I just don't really know her. And being around her stresses me out because I know she's going to say something about my gender—either on purpose or by mistake. And it doesn't really matter which she does because it hurts either way.

"Linus?" Etta calls out. Clearly, she's done, and I'm taking forever. Whoops!

"Yeah," I call back. "I'm fine." My stomach cramps again. I'm not fine.

When I get out of the bathroom, Etta is standing with her arms crossed in front of her.

"We don't have to go," she says, but I can see the disappointment in her face. "We can just get cider and hang out by the bonfire." Honestly, that seems great to me, but the way Etta says it, it sounds like a prison sentence.

"How about I go stand in line for cider while you go through the barn?" I offer. A compromise.

I can tell that Etta isn't quite sure what to do. I'm not

sure what *I* want her to do. I want to spend the whole afternoon with her, so I want her to come into the cider line with me, but I don't want her to feel like she missed out on something she wants to do because of me. That doesn't feel good either.

"Really," I say finally. Etta tilts her head, like she's waiting for me to say something else. "You go and, uh, preview the barn. See what all the scary bits are, and then . . ." I swallow. "And then I'll go in it with you, and you can warn me about all the stuff that's gonna make me freak out."

"Really?" Etta looks brighter. "Actually, that's a great idea! Plus, I'd get to do it twice."

We walk back toward the entrance to the barn. My stomach still feels unsettled. Etta waves goodbye, and I make my way to the cider line, which is shorter than I expected. I take two cups of cider over to the bonfire and place them on the bench next to me. And then, for no particular reason, I pull out my notebook and open it up to the list that Etta made about my good qualities. I read through her words, questioning if they're really true.

<u>THINGS ABOUT LINUS</u>
CARES ABOUT OTHER PEOPLE
GOOD SENSE OF HUMOR
MOM HAS A GOOD SENSE OF HUMOR

FRESH PERSPECTIVE ABOUT DOOLITTLE
EASY TO TALK TO
GOOD SMILE
GOOD HEART

Are these things true about me? I mean, Etta thinks they are. So *someone* thinks these things about me. That makes them at least a *little* true.

I start writing a list on the right side of the page, mirroring what Etta wrote about me.

THINGS ABOUT ETTA

I put the title on the opposite side of the page from the words *Things About Linus*. Then I look down the rest of my list and start imagining how those things show up in Etta.

First up. Cares about other people. Etta's whole vibe is "I don't care about you," but that's not really true. She cares about me. I think about the way that she let go of entering the haunted barn together right away, a thing she clearly really wanted to do, in order to make me feel a little better. And even now, thinking about going into the barn isn't so bad because Etta will know what's coming, and she'll protect me. So I write:

PROTECTIVE OF FRIENDS (LIKE A WOLF)

If I have a good sense of humor, it's because Etta gets the jokes. And even though she isn't much of a laugher, she found a way to tell me with our secret hand gesture. I add:

GETS JOKES (EVEN IF SHE DOESN'T LAUGH) = SMART!

I laugh at the item about my mom on the list. And quickly scrawl:

ALWAYS WILLING TO COMMIT TO A BIT (SEE THING
ABOUT MY MOM BEING FUNNY)

I draw an arrow to Etta's words about my mom having a good sense of humor.

Next, there's my fresh perspective. My new take on Doolittle might be useful, but Etta was the one who helped me find my way that first day. And she's the person who is helping me do this whole student council campaign at all. Her knowledge about how the school works is super helpful.

KNOWS A LOT ABOUT DOOLITTLE

Then there's the thing about being easy to talk to. I mean, Etta's been that way with me. Ever since I've known her. Maybe not with everyone? I don't really know. But . . . she's so interesting and fun to talk with. So I add that.

FUN TO TALK TO

The next one is easy. Etta's counter to my good smile is:

SUPERCOOL DAGGER GLARE

This last one is easy too:

GOOD HEART

"Whatcha working on?" A voice jerks me out of my thoughtful state, pulling me away from my notebook and back into reality.

And there, standing in front of me, is Marigold.

"Marigold?" I say. My voice sounds shaky and unsure. Like I can't believe she's here. Which I kind of can't.

"Hi, Linus." She smiles at me. She's wearing a flannel shirt with a puffy vest over it and a pair of black leggings with tall brown boots. In the back of my mind, I can imagine Etta calling the look Pumpkin Spice Basic, but it suits Marigold. It's hard to think of anything not suiting Marigold. I blush. This girl is going to think I'm always sunburnt around her. At least it's getting darker outside. Maybe she can't see.

"What are you doing here?" I ask.

"Oh, I always come to opening night at Dover's. It's, like, a tradition." Her eyes dart away, like she's not quite comfortable. Did I make her feel uncomfortable? "What's that?" she asks again, pointing at my notebook.

"Oh, nothing. Just . . . I'm not much of a scary person." Well, that didn't really make sense.

"Yeah, I don't find you scary at all."

"Okay. Good," I say. Why is it impossible to come up with halfway decent things to say to Marigold?! At this point, I would settle for a full sentence that doesn't contain the words *okay, good,* or *cool.* "I mean, I'm not into all of the scary stuff." I'll take it.

"Oh. Then why are you here?" She tilts her head, looking at me with what seems like genuine curiosity.

"My friend invited me. From school."

"You mean Etta?" There's something odd about the way she says Etta's name. I mean, she doesn't make a face. Or do anything that I can exactly describe. But there's something about the way she says it that gets my Spidey-sense tingling.

"Yeah. Etta is really into this stuff. And I'm . . ." I almost say that I'm into petting farms, but I stop just in time.

"So you're tagging along, even though you're not really into it?" She wrinkles her nose. It's kind of cute, except I don't think what she's saying is actually that nice.

I mean, she's right. I'm not really into the haunted barn. But I've had a good time. I get to spend the evening with Etta—making jokes, talking about whatever we want to talk about. "The car ride was fun." My attempt to justify my presence sounds lackluster. Like I don't really believe it myself. But I do.

"Hey, Linus! So, I think—" Etta is talking as she walks up to us but freezes as soon as she sees Marigold.

"Hey, Etta. I was just chatting with Linus while you, uh, went in the haunted barn without him."

"Well, I was previewing it for him," Etta says, her words clipped and icy.

"Uh, yeah," I agree. Though I'm confused by Etta's tone.

"Oh? How was it?" Marigold asks.

"I mean, I think Linus can handle it."

"Great. Then let's all go together!" Marigold's voice is bright. I swallow. I mean, I guess being in there with Marigold will be a good incentive to act braver than I really feel, right? My heart is beating wildly because of her. Definitely not because I'm terrified by whatever is in the barn.

"You know, now that I think about it, there's this

thing with scary clowns; you said those freak you out, right, Linus?"

I mean, I didn't say that. But they do freak me out. Don't they freak everyone out? I nod, my mouth dry.

"So," Etta continues, "we'll sit this one out. Have fun though." Etta gives a kind of salute-and-shoo to Marigold and grabs my hand to tug me toward the entrance of the petting farm. I look at Marigold, who rolls her eyes.

"See you at school on Tuesday, Linus. Feel free to text if you need any help with homework," she says, and then turns toward the haunted barn and joins a group of girls who are huddled around waiting for her.

Feel free to text? *Me!* Like I need more of an invitation. And even though I'm confused about the obvious coolness between Marigold and Etta, I smile as I fall in step with Etta for another grand tour of the sad petting farm.

14
Etta

LINUS KEEPS FINDING WAYS TO SURPRISE ME. NOT IN A JUMP-SCARE WAY. IN A HEARTWARMING WAY. GROSS.

Linus and I spend the car ride home preparing for the Q&A session. We make a list of possible other candidates in the eighth grade. We think about potential questions. We create a series of three important points that Linus should make sure his audience hears him say.

Linus cares about Doolittle.

Linus cares about you.

Linus wants to make Doolittle a place where you feel comfortable.

That last one was the hard one to come up with. We struggled to figure out the last word. We went back and forth, round and round. Happy? No, it felt weird and totally unreasonable to say Linus was going to make you feel happy about school. Respected? That's too much like something an adult would say. Ready to learn? Barf.

When we're about fifteen minutes from home, Mom tells Linus he should call his parents to make sure they're home. He does. I try to tune out his conversation; it feels private to listen to someone talking on the phone when the other person isn't on speaker. But it's hard not to hear.

"Hi, Mom, we'll be home in fifteen minutes . . . Oh, um, that's nice of her to offer . . . I mean, yeah, of course, that's fine." His voice sounds tired. "No, I don't think she'd want to come . . . Yeah, I'll ask her . . . Love you too."

"Who's her?" I ask. Out loud. Something I one-thousand-and-ten percent did not intend to do. But here we are.

"Oh, her is you, actually. My mom wanted to invite you to dinner with my grandma tomorrow." The car is dark, and I can't really see Linus's face too well. But I can hear the dullness in his voice.

"You don't want me to come?" Is . . . Am I embarrassing? I don't like the way my throat is feeling tight, so I say, "Do I embarrass you, Linus?" I mean the comment to be a joke. But there's this part of me that feels kind of guilty because we wouldn't even *be* friends if it weren't for the bet with Marigold. Who actually might think I'm embarrassing. I don't know. I never got those answers.

My eyes feel kind of hot, and I'm looking down at my hands and fiddling with the friendship bracelet on my wrist when I feel one of Linus's hands settle over mine. He slowly squeezes.

"Of course not," he says. Quietly. There's something electric in our touch. I can feel the air humming around us, full of unspoken words. I sit still. Because it's clear that Linus has something to say, and he's not sure how to say it. Or even if he should try. And I really, really want him to try.

"I don't want you to think I've been keeping this a secret, okay?"

I nod. I think about making a joke about how we've only known each other for a few days, and that isn't long enough for deception. And then I remember that I've managed to pull it off just fine. Guilt settles around me. It's even worse because this moment feels so serious and earnest.

"I'm trans. When I was born, I was named after my grandma. So interacting with her is kind of weird. Because she forgets that I'm Linus. Or she doesn't want to know that I am. And it's just really uncomfortable. I don't want you to be in the middle of that."

I blink. Of all the things Linus could have told me . . . this was not on my radar. At all. Linus is . . . well, he's a *boy*. Why would it occur to me to think he wasn't? Not that he isn't. That's not what I mean. He *is* a boy. He's a boy! I say the words over and over in my head. I'm like a broken record.

"I see you processing." My eyes snap up to Linus's and I see that he looks . . . sad? Scared? His eyebrows are drawn together, and his eyes look kind of wet, like he might cry.

"No," I sputter. "I mean, yes. It's a . . ." I stop myself before I say "a lot." I take a breath. "I don't want to say the wrong thing."

Linus nods. Still sad.

I take another breath and try again. "Sorry. This really isn't about me," I say. "I'll keep saying stuff until I get it right, okay?"

Linus's eyes flick to mine.

"I'm really glad you told me. But I'm also . . . It doesn't really change much for me, I guess. You're still my friend—"

I hear Linus gasp.

"What? Was that the wrong thing?"

"No. It was the very right thing."

Linus falls toward me, wrapping his arms around my waist and tumbling into a massive bear hug between our two seats in the back of my mom's van. I start to laugh. Really laugh. Loud and hard. I hear Linus laughing too. We're just a ball of howling laughter. Like Linus's revelation just made us both feel a bit more at ease. A bit more comfortable.

"Comfortable!" I say out loud as it floats across my head.

"What?"

"That's what you want. At least I think it is. You want

to make Doolittle a place where you—where everyone feels comfortable."

"Oh. Yeah. I . . . guess. I guess that *is* what I want."

Linus smiles at me, but as we drive, the lights flashing on his face make it look like a grimace. Horror movies sometimes use that strobe effect to disorient the audience. Up until now I felt so sure about my course. Win the bet with Marigold and head off to Nova, and don't care about the collateral damage. But here I am looking at the smile on Linus's face, and the course doesn't feel so clear. What if he gets hurt? And what if I'm the reason?

15
Linus

I KEEP MANAGING TO FIND NEW WAYS TO EARN A GOLD MEDAL IN THE AWKWARD OLYMPICS.

Despite my insistence that she absolutely does not need to come to dinner on Monday, Etta somehow manages to finagle a seat at the table with my family at Tiny Thai, a restaurant that immediately makes good on the first part of its name and hopefully makes good on the second part soon.

"You know, I've actually never had Thai before," says Etta, filling the silence that falls over the table after we order.

"Oh, it's one of Linus's favorites," says Dad.

"It's nice that there are vegan options," says Etta. "I'm always a little worried when I go to a new restaurant."

"I'm surprised by that," says Mom. "I would think most places would be able to handle that kind of a request. It's pretty trendy."

"Well, we're still in Ohio." Etta's voice has a bit of a bite to it.

"Etta isn't doing it to be trendy," I say defensively. I don't like the implication that Etta is jumping on some bandwagon. And even if she was, is that such a bad thing? "Some of it has to do with allergies. Some of it is animal rights. You've been a vegan for a long time, right?"

"Since third grade," Etta says mildly, giving me the side-eye. Then she looks down and pulls her phone out of her pocket and begins to type. I look at my parents, who pretend not to notice. We're all busy being polite when my phone buzzes in my pocket. I pull it out.

Etta: u stood up for me just fine

"Linus, no phones at the table," Mom says. I look over at Etta, who snickers, but I don't rat her out because a friend wouldn't do that. And I'm pretty sure my parents wouldn't talk to Etta the same way they talk to me. The way they would sometimes talk to Olive—like she was their kid too. Etta is new to them.

"So, how's school going for you two?" Dad asks.

Etta looks over at me with an expression that plainly says she very much does not want to talk about school. Of course, I'm not entirely sure what Etta *would* want to talk to my parents about. The weather? The latest sports-ball scores? How long it takes for paint to dry?

"Uh, it's fine. It's school," I say, trying to move the

conversation away from this. I'm just not sure what I'm hoping to move it toward.

"Etta, what do you like to do outside of school?" Mom asks. *No, Mom. Stop. She clearly isn't into it. Let's not drive my friend away, please and thank you!*

"Did you tell your parents about student council?" Etta diverts the attention away from her and over to me.

I kick her under the table.

I haven't told them. I'm not really sure why. Maybe it's because I haven't wanted to talk to them as much. Honestly, it seems more likely than not that I'll say something that they wouldn't like.

"Are you running for student council, Liney?" Mom asks. She seems pleasantly surprised, the smile on her lips genuine.

Even though it's nice to feel this rush of support, I feel uneasy with the attention of the whole table on me. "Yeah, Etta convinced me it would be a good idea," I say, trying to shift attention away from me and onto anything else.

"And Etta didn't want to run herself?" Dad asks.

"Nope." She pops the *P* at the end of *nope* in a way that plainly indicates she won't be saying any more on the subject. There's another long, awkward pause.

"Well, that sounds lovely," Mom says. "Just imagine, this could be the beginning of an illustrious career in politics!"

I want to snort because I don't know that much about politics outside of middle school, but what I do know doesn't sound very fun. I don't snort, though, 'cause Mom is trying to pay me a compliment.

Another pause. Mom's smile starts to falter, and she turns to Grandma. My stomach lurches because I really don't want to hear what my grandmother has to say about my chances in the student council election. Instead, Mom mercifully changes the subject.

"Mom, did you want to tell Linus and Etta about the movie we saw this weekend?"

"It was called *The Staff*." I've never heard of this movie, but Etta perks up right away.

"No way! Did you like it?" Etta leans in. My grandmother has her full attention. I feel kind of territorial? Like, I want this meal to be pleasant and all, but also Etta is *my* friend. Wait, am I jealous of my grandmother?!

"The plot was nonsensical at times," Grandma says.

"I heard it's super gory!" Etta chips in.

Oh, it's a horror movie. No wonder I've never heard of it. I lean back in my chair, cross my arms, and watch as the pair of them debate the merits of gore in horror movies.

"By American standards, I guess. We've got nothing on Japanese films," Grandma says matter-of-factly. Now they've moved on to a detailed breakdown of their favorite horror movies. When I look over at my parents, they look just as confused as I feel. Though maybe not as jealous.

"I secretly wanted Claire and Doug to name their child Annabelle when she was born," Grandma says, indicating me.

It gets quiet. Really quiet. For a long time.

This is the awkward pause to end all awkward pauses. I slump even lower in my seat and close my eyes.

I wait for my parents to say something. Surely, after I spoke to Dad, he'll jump in and help when Grandma made such an obvious error in front of Etta, in front of someone new.

Etta looks at me and raises her eyebrows. It's weird how looks can say so much with so little. Because Etta only had to raise her eyebrows and I know she's saying three things at once: (1) Wow, I don't like your grandmother right now, (2) You wanna say something? (3) I got your back. And even with a look that says all that, I lower myself even farther so my eyes are even with the edge of the table. I should say something. Etta thinks I should say something. *I* think I should say something. I should say something.

I slowly uncrumple my body so I'm sitting up with my arms still crossed over my chest. "Uh, it's a good thing Etta already knows I'm trans, or this would be really awkward," I finally say. Which honestly is kind of funny because the awkwardness at the table is its own living thing. My comment's not a correction, but it breaks the tension. Almost immediately, our waitress swoops in with our food, and we all silently agree to move on and slurp down our pad Thai.

My phone buzzes again. I look at my parents, who are busy eating, before checking it.

Etta: we'll work on it

I know what *it* is. We'll work on me standing up for myself. It feels a little more possible with a friend by my side.

—

I hand in my nomination form first thing on Tuesday morning so I don't overthink it and back out. I spent more of the night after dinner going over the questions with Etta, who seemed to vacillate between caring very much about what I wrote and thinking that the form didn't really matter.

I don't even get a chance to survey the available seats in the classroom before Marigold is at my side, guiding me to take the seat next to her in the front row.

"Did I see you give a nomination form to Mr. Todd?" she asks. I turn approximately the color of a fire engine and try to hide it as I stuff my backpack under the desk next to Marigold's.

"Uh, yeah. I might . . . I might see what it's about."

"That's great!" Marigold smiles at me. My face gets impossibly hotter.

"Yeah," I say. I wish I had something better to say. Like a joke or something. Maybe not a joke. Maybe that wouldn't land. It takes me a moment to realize that while I'm thinking of the perfect line to impress Marigold, she's been talking.

"—so we'll see how it all shakes out."

Oh, shoot. I missed something. I nod.

As Mr. Todd starts class, I look around for Etta and jump when I realize she's sitting at the desk behind me, her head on her desk and her arms wrapped around it, her green hair forming a messy nest. Huh, I didn't notice her come in.

"Good morning, everyone—and an especially good morning to those of you who turned in your nomination forms!" Mr. Todd smiles in my direction when he says that special *good morning.* "If you're still on the fence, I'm accepting nominations through the end of the day. And tomorrow, we'll have a question-and-answer session with candidates at our eighth-grade assembly."

Marigold raises her hand.

"Yes, Marigold."

"Is there anything candidates can do to prepare for the session?" she asks. She looks over at me, like she asked the question for my benefit. I smile at her and turn to Mr. Todd to hear the answer.

"Think about the things that make you a good representative," says Mr. Todd. "Sure, you might want to consider the sweeping changes you would make to the school, but at the end of the day, your peers are voting for a person, not a promise of a two-month winter vacation. Which isn't going to happen, by the way, no matter what anyone says at the Q&A session tomorrow!"

The class groans.

"So, I would say: Think about how you want to present yourself, and remember, the best approach with these sorts of things is always honesty. Anything else?"

I have a bunch of questions about what student council does, but no one else raises their hand, so I don't either. Better to just blend in. Even if I'm going to be standing out at the Q&A tomorrow morning.

It's about halfway through class when I realize nature is calling, so I raise my hand and get permission to go to the bathroom. Mr. Todd waves me out, and I make my way to the closest restroom, where the literal worst thing that happens to me every month happens. When I go to wipe, my TP comes back with a red smear. The sight of blood makes my heart race. I have supplies—I've been getting my period for two years now, and each occurrence manages to be terrible—but I don't have supplies *here*. My small zippered case filled with tampons and pads is safely in the bottom of my backpack, which I shoved under my desk when I abso-tively posi-lutely lost my cool while talking to Marigold earlier.

Crap.

Crap. Crap. Crap.

I have my phone. I think about . . . what? Texting my mom? *Hey, Mom, I'm in the boys' bathroom on the second floor, please come and rescue me!* No. Not that.

Hot tears are streaming down my face as I lean over to the toilet paper dispenser and pull out an unholy amount of the stuff. I fold it carefully and place it in my underwear. Hopefully that will hold.

When I get back to the classroom, Mr. Todd is still talking, so I can't be super stealth getting to my seat, let alone grabbing my backpack and leaving the room again.

"What's up, Linus? The Articles of Confederation not doing it for you today?" I wince. I think Mr. Todd is trying to be cute, but I'm about to burst into tears in the middle of class.

"I . . . I just need to go to the bathroom," I say. My voice shakes on the *oom* of *bathroom*.

"Again? Weren't you just there?" Mr. Todd asks with a chuckle.

"Yeah . . . I . . . just need to go back to the bathroom,"

I correct. Maybe I can just . . . state what it is I need. And I'll get to go.

"Yeah . . . no dice, Linus. The bell will ring in twenty. I think you can hold it until passing time." And then Mr. Todd turns back to whatever he was talking about. The Articles of Confederation, I guess.

The likelihood of me being able to pay attention to anything but the way the tops of my legs are pressed together while silently praying that blood doesn't seep into the seat of my jeans is pretty much nonexistent. Fortunately, I've got a hoodie on over my shirt today, so I can take that off quickly when I stand up and tie it around my waist. I've seen pictures of my parents where they did that. There's one of the two of them at the top of a mountain. It was when Mom and Dad were younger—before me. In the photo, my mom has her arms wrapped around my dad, her lips pressed against his cheek in a kissing pose. My dad has both of his fists in the air in a *We did it!* kind of pose. Both of them look exhausted but happy. And both of them have their sweatshirts tied around their waists. Like the hike started to overheat them as they got farther and farther up the mountain.

I look at the clock. There's still nineteen minutes left. Will my TP pad last that long? I try to think of something to distract me. Anything. But not even imagining having the perfect conversation with Marigold keeps me from internally freaking out.

16
Etta

IS IT HARD TO DISTRACT EIGHTH GRADERS WHO DON'T WANT TO BE IN CIVICS CLASS? NO. BUT I'M STILL REALLY GOOD AT IT.

I'm stewing over the betrayal of Linus and Marigold sitting together when Linus comes back from the bathroom looking panicked. He gets extra twitchy when Mr. Todd says he can't go to the bathroom a second time.

I don't know what's going on, but if Linus needs to go to the bathroom, I'm getting him to the bathroom. That's what friends do. The only thing I can think of is a distraction, so I pull out my phone and pull up the most anti-school movie soundtrack I can think of: *The Breakfast Club*. I connect my phone through the Bluetooth to the screen on the board, and blast Simple Minds.

Everyone jumps. I immediately lean forward to Linus and say, "Go!" He doesn't hesitate, just grabs his backpack and slinks out of the room without anyone noticing. I mean, how could they? Mr. Todd is fumbling with the remote for the screen, and a surprising number of eighth graders are singing along.

I quickly text Linus to make sure he's okay, then shut off my phone and hide it away. The music stops abruptly, but the damage is done. The class is off track, and it will be impossible to get back on. The perfect crime.

After class, I check my phone. Linus has responded with a series of shark emojis, which makes me worried he might be turning into a shark. I decide to wait by his locker to make sure that he doesn't have a fin or gills or something.

When Linus sees me, he smiles.

"Thanks," he says. "I don't know how you did it, but thank you."

"Did what?" I ask, grinning. "Now, what does this mean?" I hold up my phone.

"It's shark week," Linus says quietly.

"Um, Shark Week is in summer. And it's the best week of the year."

"Well, this one happens once a month, and it's the worst," Linus responds.

Finally, I get it. "Oh!"

"Yeah." Linus pushes his hair out of his eyes. "I was caught without supplies."

"I thought there were pads in the bathrooms?" I ask.

"Maybe in the *girls'* bathrooms." Linus gives me a pointed look.

"Look, that's something you could do something about if you are elected to student council!" I say. I mean, wouldn't it be great if Linus getting elected meant the school was better for trans kids?

"Maybe . . . ," Linus says. He sounds like he's really considering it. "See you at lunch?"

"Of course."

Linus waves and heads down the hall to his next class.

The next morning, Linus is wearing a black button-down shirt with a shark bow tie for the Q&A session. The eighth graders are all sitting in the auditorium. A few other kids look more on the dressed-up side, but it's hard to tell at a glance who is running for student council and who is just fancy. Anyone and everyone (other than me) could wind up doing the Q&A, for all I know. I mean, I doubt it, based on Mr. Todd's earlier pleas that someone—anyone—take the nomination form. But still. There could have been a late surge.

"Hello, eighth graders!" Mr. Todd says into the microphone. A few people yell, "Hey!" back. Most of the eighth graders ignore him. I would have been one of them a week ago. Now I'm next to Linus, who is stick-straight in his chair. I rest my hand on Linus's arm and squeeze every so often. We've got this. He's got this.

17

Linus

I GET NERVOUS TALKING TO PEOPLE I DON'T KNOW ONE-ON-ONE.
I'M NOT SURE WHAT MADE ME THINK THAT TALKING TO THEM
ONSTAGE WOULD SOMEHOW BE LESS TERRIFYING.

"Before we get to the main event, I want to remind you of how this works. I will call up the candidates and ask them each a starter question. Then I'll open the floor to peer questions. You may not address a particular candidate; your questions should be something all candidates could speak to. As a reminder, we are looking for two boys and two girls to represent the eighth grade."

I blink. I don't remember Mr. Todd saying that before. Why does gender have anything to do with this? I mean, I get the idea that they want to have a diverse group of people representing each grade, but this feels like such a basic way to achieve that. Plus, gender isn't binary! Etta squeezes my arm, pulling me out of my thoughts.

"Without further ado, I present your eighth-grade student council candidates: Kelli DeBris, Harrison Levi,

Annie Rose, Skye Schuler, Marigold Stimpson, and Linus Stout."

"There's only two boys!" Etta whispers to me, hushed excitement caking her voice. "You're gonna be on student council! Now go up there and kill it!"

I try to find some feeling of excitement to match Etta's, but it just isn't there. This doesn't feel right.

There's a smattering of applause as we make our way to the stage. As I walk up, I slide my hand into my back pocket, where I've put the list that Etta made about me (and the one I made about her). It's like a security blanket, reminding me that there are lots of good things about me. Lots of reasons for people to vote for me. To like me.

When we get to the stage, the candidates stand awkwardly in a line. There are no podiums. Just two microphones that Mr. Todd is holding.

"All right," says Mr. Todd. "Let's warm up these candidates. Marigold, I'll start with you. What is your favorite holiday, and why?"

He hands the second microphone to Marigold, who says, "When I was younger, my birthday was my favorite, but now that I'm older, I guess my favorite is a birthday that everyone celebrates: America's birthday. So, the Fourth of July is my answer!"

I wrinkle my nose. I mean, that's a silly question,

and her answer sounds polished . . . but it isn't, like, a great answer. At least, I don't think it's so great. It's weird because I've spent the past four days thinking about all the ways that Marigold *is* great. So thinking of her as something-less-than-great seems strange. She's something other than this unattainable crush. She's a human. A human who sometimes has bad takes.

Mr. Todd goes down the line, asking about favorite ice cream flavors, the last book someone read and what they thought about it, favorite color . . . I try to keep breathing. This part isn't hard. Just . . . be honest. Isn't that what Mr. Todd said to do? Just be honest. My heart is thundering in my ears, making it hard for me to hear the questions and the answers.

"And finally, Linus Stout." Suddenly the words are clear and much too loud. "Where's your favorite place to get a slice of pizza in the metro-Toledo area?"

"Oh," I say. Because I don't have an answer. I thought this was supposed to be easy! "Well . . . I . . ."

Mr. Todd seems to realize his misstep at that moment. "Sorry, Linus. I forgot that you just moved here, I'll—"

"No, it's okay," I say, pushing through the slight hiccup of panic that threatens to erupt in my chest and grabbing the microphone. A high-pitched squeal pierces out of the sound system, and everyone screams and covers their ears. In the moment of chaos, I look out into the audience and find Etta, who is no longer slumped in her seat. She's sitting up and looking at me, nodding—just a little—to encourage me.

"All right, all right, settle down," Mr. Todd says. "Linus, you were saying?"

"You're right," I say into the microphone, hating the way my voice sounds over the speakers. "I don't have an answer. I haven't really had time to do an in-depth Ohio-based pizza study." A few kids chuckle. I stand up straighter. "But I can tell all of you that if you go to New York City someday, you should definitely get a slice of pizza from Coronet's on 110th!"

"Great. Thanks, Linus." Mr. Todd gives me a wink. "And now it's time for some real hardballs from all of you!" He gestures out to the audience. "Anyone got a burning question for your would-be reps?"

A grand total of two hands go up. Mr. Todd makes his way to one of the students, handing him the microphone.

"What's your stance on ordering delivery for lunch? Like from restaurants."

I look down at the microphone in my hand, but I can't think of an answer. There's a long silence, and then Mr. Todd finally says, "Anyone want to take a first crack at this one?"

A girl with long black hair—Kelli, I think—raises her hand. I run the mic over to her and drop it into her hands like it's a hot potato.

"I don't really see a problem with it. I mean, if you

want something else for lunch and you have the money to pay for it, why shouldn't you have it?"

There's some applause and a fist in the air from the original question-asker. I guess that's the right answer.

Marigold waves her hand like she has something to add, and the microphone makes its way to her.

"Respectfully, I think it should probably be more of a discussion. Not everyone has access to money to get takeout every day. Or even a phone." A few people chuckle. "I mean it. Not everyone has a phone."

"Who doesn't have a phone?" Kelli asks. She looks at Marigold, then the audience. No one answers, though a few students hoot in response.

"That's not really the point. I'm just saying that just because you *can* doesn't mean you *should*. And we should be making space for that discussion."

I raise my hand now. Because, to my surprise, I have something to add. And because I want to support Marigold.

"I agree with Marigold. I think it's worth having a discussion. I will also say that the school cafeteria works hard to have allergy-friendly options." I think about how Etta heads into the kitchen each day to get her rundown about what she can eat and what she should avoid. "And there are some foods, like peanuts, that might be really dangerous for people in our school. I guess I'm saying, let's be thoughtful."

There's light applause. I look out into the crowd, and Etta gives me a thumbs-up. A genuine, honest-to-goodness thumbs-up. From Etta!

"Anyone else?" Mr. Todd asks in his mic. "No? Okay, I think Angela had a question."

He walks over to Angela, who is sitting in the front row. She says, "What parties do you think the school should host?"

There are a few tentative answers from the candidates. A party for Halloween. A spring fling dance. No one seems to really know how to answer this one.

I look out at Etta, who holds up three fingers. This was the signal we decided on for her to help me remember to stay on message.

I care about Doolittle.

I care about you.

I want to make Doolittle a place where you feel comfortable.

I swallow and raise my hand. The mic makes its way to me.

"I think *when* the parties are is less important than, like, *what* the parties are. I think it would be really cool if there were different activities. Like, yeah, there can be music and dancing, but what about, like, a movie? Or board games?" A few people nod. "Or a Pokémon tournament?" Two boys emphatically support this proposal. "Part of my job as a student council representative would be to make everyone feel comfortable at Doolittle. I think the way we plan parties can be part of that." Again, there's applause. A few more people make comments. Marigold adds that an allergy-friendly ice cream bar might be a lot of fun. I almost say that we would need to make sure that there is a dairy-free option for people like Etta, but I hold it in.

"Any more questions?" Mr. Todd asks as the party answers wind down.

A short boy stretches his hand so high in the air it looks like he might pull a muscle.

"Maximus, yes!" Mr. Todd makes his way to the boy, and I try not to laugh at his ironic name.

"I'm wondering what made each of you decide to do this," says Maximus into the mic.

My heart starts to race, and every thought I had runs out of my head. What business *do* I have wanting to do this?

The microphone starts down the line. The answers are generic. Nothing too earth-shattering.

"I want to make good changes."

"I want to make middle school better."

Surely, I can say something nondescript. But then the mic gets to Marigold. She looks at . . . me?!

"There are a lot of good reasons to want to be on student council. I agree with everything my opponents have said. But I also think we have a chance to work with a great group of people."

Did I mention that she's looking at *me* when she says this? Like . . . I don't want to put words in her mouth, but it sounds like she's saying that she wants to do student council to spend time with me. Which . . . is bananas and fantastic. Banastic. I mean, sure, her holiday answer kind of sucked . . . but . . . this. Well, it more than makes up for it. She's back to being perfect-crush-material Marigold.

Another candidate answers, and the mic makes its way to me.

"Um . . . as you all know, I'm new. So . . . for me, this is a chance to get to know the school and . . . maybe do something good."

Oof. Not great, Linus. Way to biff it!

There's another long silence. I seem to be really good at prompting those. I can feel my ears getting hot as Mr. Todd makes his way back to the stage.

"Okay, well, then . . . I'll wrap up by saying that there are only two boys in the running for the eighth grade, so congrats to Harrison and Linus!" I can hear Etta whoop from her seat. I'm glad she's happy, or maybe proud. But I don't feel the same way. Something about this doesn't really feel right. I mean, I want to be on student council, I think, but if I'm not one of the top four, I shouldn't just win by default. "And as for the girls, you'll have a chance to vote during lunch to—"

"Mr. Todd," I say, stepping forward and lifting the mic that is still in my hand to my mouth. "Can I say something?"

"Uh, well, the Q&A session is wrapping up, Linus. I really think—"

"It's important," I say. I give him what I hope is a meaningful look. It must work because he steps back and yields the stage to me.

"I just wanted to say . . . I don't think I should automatically be on student council because I'm a boy and only two boys ran."

I can almost hear Etta screaming, "WHAT ARE YOU DOING?" So I make a point of *not* looking in her direction as I go on. I look to the back of the auditorium, where I see Mx. B is standing with their arms crossed. I take a deep breath, even more sure about what I'm about to say.

"I get that you want a good mix of people representing the grade, but . . . there's more to diversity than just boy and girl. Heck, there's more to gender than boy and girl. So I just respectfully ask that we reconsider the policy and have a vote with all six of us on the ballot for the four spots."

I go to hand the microphone to Mr. Todd and have every intention of going back to my spot in the line, but

Marigold stops me. She comes over, takes my hand, and brings me back to the front of the stage.

Then she takes the mic from my other hand and says, "I agree." Her hand feels warm and solid in mine. I worry for a second that my palm might erupt with a Pacific Ocean amount of sweat, but somehow it stays mostly dry.

Next, Annie steps forward. She doesn't take the mic, just yells out, "I agree."

Then the rest of the girls chime in with "I agree." Only poor Harrison, who barely said anything all assembly and probably knows that this shift means he won't be on student council at all, hangs back. After a few longer-than-usual seconds, Harrison, too, joins the line.

"I agree," he says with slightly less enthusiasm than the others.

Marigold turns to the audience and, using the microphone as a baton, conducts the entire eighth grade to stand. And . . . miraculously, they all do. I stare out into the audience, my mouth hanging open, as an enthusiastic chorus of "I agree" echoes back to us. It's not begrudging or lackluster. It's powerful. Like everyone out there is on our—*my* side. I'm still staring out into the sea of eighth graders nodding back at me when Marigold lifts the microphone back up and says, "I think the 'I agrees' have it." She gives my hand a little squeeze before letting go. My chest swells, and even though I feel like I might cry, I'm not embarrassed or worried about it. I took a risk, and it didn't end in disaster or second-guessing. I feel like, for the first time in a long time, I'm in harmony with the world around me.

"I agree," Mr. Todd says into his own microphone.

The entire eighth grade erupts into cheers. Marigold turns to me and smiles.

"Great job, Linus!" she calls out over the screams. I smile back at her. My heart is pounding in my chest. But not from nerves or stress or anxiety. Not even because I got to hold Marigold's hand for about thirty seconds. It's that I'm happy. I'm completely and fully happy. And it's amazing.

18
Etta

VOTE FOR LINUS. OR ELSE.

It's hard to know if I'm pissed at Linus or really proud of him. Because that little golden retriever nerd just pulled off a grade-A impressive move . . . that has the potential to seriously mess up my chances of winning my bet with Marigold . . . and also puts my shot at Nova in jeopardy. So, yeah, it's a mix.

But Linus is hugging me within two seconds of the Q&A wrapping up, which is very endearing, particularly since it means he managed to pull away from Marigold's moony eyes and grabby hands. Point to Etta.

"Wasn't that incredible?" he asks over the chatter of the excited crowd.

And because I don't want to crush him (and because it truthfully was), I say, "Absolutely."

Inside, however, I'm a nervous wreck until lunch. Because Linus might have caused some excitement at the Q&A, but there's no guarantee that will translate to cold, hard votes. And you can't be student council president if you aren't on student council in the first place.

When lunch arrives, I plant myself at the table next to Mr. Todd's "voting booth" and mutter "Vote for Linus" under my breath as students walk in. It's more of a subliminal message than an actual one because I might fully support Linus in his quest for student council domination (and the subsequent Etta-over-Marigold domination), but I still have a reputation to preserve! I can't find Linus at lunch, which hopefully means he's doing some last-minute campaigning. Kissing babies. Making promises he has no intention of keeping. The usual.

It isn't until halfway through Spanish that Mr. Todd's voice crackles over the PA system.

"Sorry for this brief interruption. I would like to announce the winners of the race for student council. In the sixth grade, we have Isaya Robbins, Lily Rosenthal, Barnaby Tucker, and Franny Zhu." Why is he starting with sixth grade?! "In the seventh grade, there's Greg Gerwig, Sean Moffatt, Kelly Moby, and Monica Sazmatongolaz." COULD THIS BE TAKING ANY LONGER?! HOW ARE WE NOT AT THE EIGHTH GRADE YET?! "And for eighth grade, we have Kelli DeBris, Annie Rose, Marigold Stimpson . . ." Of course . . . last . . . "and . . ." Please. *Please let it be Linus. Please let us still be in this.* "Linus Stout. Thank you for your attention."

I let out a breath. We did it. We're . . . well, *Linus* is

in student council. Phase one is complete. So now we have to move on to phase two. Get him elected student council president.

So why don't I feel any better?

By the time math rolls around, I think I've figured out that the reason I'm not totally satisfied by Linus's win is that the work isn't done yet. Yeah, he's on student council . . . but he hasn't been elected president! Heck, I don't even know if he realizes that's an option.

In math, I wait for Linus outside the classroom door, and we hug tightly as soon as he gets there, enjoying a moment of celebration together. Dave K. gives me a funny look, and I glare at him, unleashing all of the unapproachable / leave-me-alone energy I can muster.

"We did it! We did it! We did it!" Linus sings, unaware that anyone is looking at us oddly.

"*You* did it," I say. Because . . . what did I do, really? Not much. Besides, I want to pump him up. Make him realize that he can be a leader. *The* leader. *The president.*

"I wouldn't even be running if it weren't for you!"

And I wouldn't have asked you to if it weren't for Marigold and Nova. The thought floats across my head. I shiver. I hate that it's making this moment ugly. That it's taking away some of the purity of Linus's joy.

"Is everything okay?" Linus asks. Maybe he can sense something is off. All I can think is that I should ask him if he's going to run for president.

"Yeah, just, like, step one, you know?" The words sound broken. Like I don't know how to speak sentences and am just saying a bunch of random words.

"Huh?" Linus tilts his head and raises an eyebrow. I don't blame him. I barely understand me.

"I mean, Linus, your performance at the Q&A was amazing! Like, everyone has got to be thinking you're going to run for president, right?"

"Whoa! Whoa! I . . . I don't think . . ." Linus's words are kind of breathy, and he doesn't seem able to even finish his thought.

"Linus, you revolutionized the election process in real time." Maybe *revolutionized* is a little strong, but desperate times call for desperate hyperbole. "Just imagine what you could do as president. You really could . . . make the school better." What's weird is . . . I'm not just saying that. I think . . . I think I actually mean it? I think I *actually think* that Linus might make Doolittle Middle a better place.

"I don't know. Let's . . . let's just drop it," Linus says, moving to enter the classroom. I follow him. Is it really worth pushing Linus to run for president if that isn't what he wants?

After math, as I'm packing up to go home, I pull

out my phone and scroll to a number I haven't seen in about three months. I press the name, and a text thread pops up. The last text is from June. I think we should take a break from being friends.

I take a breath and start typing.

> **Me:** Hey, M. I think we need to talk about the bet.
> Can you meet at Wilcox Dairy in ten?

I watch as the three "I'm typing" dots flash up on the screen and then disappear. After a moment, they come up again. Finally. I get a text back:

> **Marigold:** What bet?

Ugh. Does she not even remember? I've been agonizing over this for a week. Doing everything in my power to get Linus elected, and Marigold doesn't even bother to remember that *she* bet me to do it?

> **Marigold:** the Linus on student council thing?
> **Marigold:** sure

Now she remembers. Ugh. I squint at my phone . . . think about what it would take to just crush the whole thing. Instead, I put my energy into running to Wilcox Dairy, which is about five blocks from school. I'm pretty winded by the time I get to the picnic tables lined up along the sidewalk of the dairy. It's not really busy yet because the elementary school doesn't get out for another hour. That's the real ice cream–eating crowd.

I sit down on one of the picnic tables that is painted pale blue with daisies all over it, continue to gasp for air, and collect my thoughts. I pull out my phone and click on my browser app—the website for Nova comes flashing up on the screen. For a moment, I feel this longing. For when Nova was the only thing I thought I wanted. But now it's complicated. Linus has made it complicated. And even though I try to act unfeeling and over-it-all, I can't keep doing this thing that might hurt my friend. I still want to go to Nova, but I know what I have to do. I need to tell Marigold the bet is off. Even if she doesn't remember it. I need to do it.

For me.

And for Linus.

19
Linus

JUST BECAUSE TWO GIRLS ARE FIGHTING, IT DOESN'T AUTOMATICALLY MEAN THEY ARE FIGHTING OVER <u>YOU</u>!

Mr. Todd flags me down as I'm heading to my locker to get my things.

"Hey, Linus, I'm talking to all the eighth-grade reps about running for president. Do you have a minute?"

"Sure, let me text my mom and let her know," I say. I pull out my phone as I follow Mr. Todd to his classroom.

"So, Linus, first of all. Congratulations. That was an impressive showing at this morning's Q&A." It's weird, but Mr. Todd seems genuinely impressed. I don't know if I've ever impressed an adult before.

"Thanks," I say.

"Yes, there was something inspiring about getting the whole auditorium to chant 'I agree' . . ." I almost cut in to say that *I* didn't do that. That really Marigold did that. "But what really impressed me was your thoughtful answers. I hope you'll consider running for president."

"Me?" I ask. Sure, Etta made a comment about me

running for president, but I don't know. It didn't feel like she was serious. But a teacher saying I should do it? Especially a teacher who is impressed by me? That feels different.

"Yes, you! You have good ideas. And you get the people around you to think. Not to mention, you listen. It's a winning combination." Mr. Todd chuckles. "That's not a bad slogan."

I think about my work with Etta. How we pulled together my three speaking points. "Well, I've been going with 'I care about Doolittle, I care about you, I want to make Doolittle a place where you feel comfortable.'"

"Hm . . . It's a little wordy. But it's got heart."

I shove my hand into my back pocket, where my list is tucked. I've been transferring it from pocket to pocket ever since Etta and I wrote it. I think about the last item on my list and the secret list I made about Etta: good heart.

"How . . . how does running for president work?" I ask. "There isn't a boy president and girl president, is there?" I joke.

Mr. Todd laughs awkwardly. "Oh, no. Nothing like that. All four of you eighth-grade reps are eligible to run. You don't have to, mind you. But I think it would be great if you did."

"What do I have to do? To run."

"Well, you would have to let me know. By the end

of the week via email. And then on Monday you would give a speech for the whole school. Parents are invited too. I'm happy to take a look at your speech over the weekend if that's helpful. But honestly, Linus, I think you could simply repackage most of what you said at the Q&A so the whole school has a chance to get to know you. What do you think?"

"Um . . ." I'm thinking about it. I really am. And part of me wants to say yes. But part of me wonders if it's too much too soon. Like, I spent all of last year pulling away. What if I don't have the stamina to jump all in to BEING IN CHARGE OF THE GOVERNING BODY OF MY NEW SCHOOL. "Let me think about it."

"But you'll email me by Friday, right?"

"Yeah, sure."

Mr. Todd smiles at me as I walk out of the room. The hallways have cleared out, everyone either heading home or heading to whatever it is they do after school. I look around for Etta, but I don't catch sight of any strands of green, so I go to my locker to pack up.

"So, how'd it go?" Mom asks as I get into the car.

"What?" I'm distracted thinking about Etta's strange reaction to the election results. And her comment that I should be president. Is she right? Is Mr. Todd right? Is that something I should go for? I mean, I think Marigold would be a great president. Who am I to stand in the way of that? Maybe I can be vice president?

"The election!" Mom says. "Am I in the car with my very own civil servant?"

"Oh. That."

"Yes, that. Linus, I'm dying here. What happened?"

"Um, I got elected, I guess." It feels weird to say it out loud.

"You guess?" Mom gives me a sidelong glance.

"Yeah. I'm on the student council," I say. Then I break out into a big smile. I guess I kind of *like* the idea of being in charge. Of being able to help the school.

"Linus! That's great! I think my little government official deserves some ice cream."

"Please tell me you are not going to come up with a million pet names for me based on the election."

"Just a dozen or so. Don't worry about it. Ice cream? You got any hot tips on the best places to score some of that sick dairy?" She's talking in some kind of weird accent. I can't even really describe it, but I think she's trying to sound cool?

"Please don't ever speak like that again!" I say, serious, yet smiling at her.

"Fair enough. But seriously, ice cream. I need it." It's nice to be able to joke with Mom like this. Recently, it's felt like every interaction with her is about my grandmother and how I need to give her more grace or whatever.

"Etta told me about a place called Wilcox Dairy. I mean, she doesn't eat dairy, so she doesn't know first-hand if the ice cream is any good, but she said the sorbet is great. Could be worth a shot."

"Sounds good."

We use Siri to make our way to Wilcox Dairy. Mom asks questions about the Q&A; I do my best to answer her. She seems genuinely proud of me. As we pull up to the dairy, though, my words dry up because there's something weird outside.

It's Etta. And Marigold. And they look like they're fighting. Not physically. But Etta looks upset. And Marigold, she doesn't look like herself at all. She's kind of curling her lip in a sneer. I mean, I definitely noticed some weirdness between Etta and Marigold before, particularly at the haunted barn, but outright fighting? That doesn't really seem like either of them, honestly.

My stomach lurches, making me feel hot and hurt.

"Mom, I changed my mind," I say, trying to sound, I don't know, casual? I pull my seat belt back around my hips.

"What? But we're here." She smiles at me and goes to open her car door.

"Yeah, I know, I just, I don't want . . ." I'm sounding more desperate.

"Linus, you love ice cream. And we drove here to—"

I look back. Marigold has her arms crossed over her chest, and Etta is talking emphatically, gesturing with her hands. Whatever they're talking about, I don't want to get in the middle of it. I feel kind of sick thinking about them fighting. And what they might be fighting about.

"MOM!" I pretty much yell the word. She has to know something is wrong now. Even though she isn't screeching out of the driveway like we're in the middle of an action movie the way I wish she would.

She pulls out of her parking spot, and we turn down a street and start moving steadily away from the dairy.

"What was that about . . . ?" Mom asks.

"Nothing," I mumble.

"Linus . . ."

"I just saw some kids from school. I don't really want to deal with whatever is going on with them right now."

"Are kids giving you a hard time?" She's instantly worried. High Alert Mom Mode activated.

"What? No. Mom, I was just elected to student council. People seem pretty okay with me."

"Okay, well, is it that you don't want to be seen with your mother? Because—"

"Mom!"

"Okay, okay. Oh, I was going to ask, what do you think we should do for dinner with Grandma on Friday?"

I sigh. I'm half-relieved that she's not asking me

about the argument and half-disappointed that we're back to talking about Grandma.

"I don't know," I say.

"Maybe we'll just eat at our house. Have a family dinner. Maybe just us this time, so don't plan anything with Etta until after seven on Friday, okay?" She winks at me. I give a weak smile back.

—

When I get home, I run up to my room, using the classic "So much homework to do!" as an excuse. Once I get to my room, I close the door and call Etta. The phone rings three times and goes to voice mail. I hang up without leaving a message and immediately call Olive, who picks up on the first ring, like a dutiful best friend.

"Olive you!" she answers.

"Hey, Olive you! Miss you."

"Same."

I think about launching into my worries about Etta and Marigold, but I don't want it to seem like I only call Olive when I'm in crisis. When I need something.

"Hey, remember that crack you made about me running for student council?"

"Do I?"

"Well, you said something about it . . . and then I texted you—"

"Sorry, my tone must have gotten lost. I didn't mean 'Do I?' like 'Do I genuinely remember?' I meant it like 'Oh boy, do I ever remember!'"

"Ah, of course. How could the nuance have been lost in translation?"

"Truly, technology has miles to go!"

We both laugh, and then I say, "Well, I did it. And I got in!" I try to sound excited.

"What?! Linus, that's amazing. That's awesome! Part of me wants to say that it feels unexpected, except it doesn't really. You going for it is what's unexpected. Not the other people voting for you part."

I smile at her words. This is what I was hoping Etta would say.

But she didn't.

So, at least there's Olive.

"So, that's my big news," I say, wondering when I should bring up the drama. I decide to wait. "What's up with you?"

"Oh, school. And I think my dads are gonna let me get a puppy!"

"Oh, really? That would be awesome. What kind?"

"I dunno. We'll probably go to the animal shelter to find a dog we can rescue. But I've wanted a dog since forever. I think they took pity on me now that you've moved away." My chest squeezes a bit. Is Olive miserable now because of me?

"Sorry, Olive . . ."

"Oh, no, I just mean, honestly, Linus, don't worry about it. Anything else up with you? I mean other than being in charge of the entire school or whatever it is your student council does."

"Uh, I'm not still one hundred percent sure what it is we do. But, um, yeah . . . there is something else. If you have a minute."

"I've got more than a minute. What's up?"

I spill. I tell Olive about Etta—my first friend here, who is a little on the abrasive side, but loyal and funny. And about Marigold—my other friend, who is super nice and involved in the school—and how she'll be on student council with me. Olive sniffs out right away that I have a crush on Marigold. Which I begrudgingly admit because what's the point of lying to Olive about it? Then I talk about the interaction at the haunted barn and the weird vibes I got there. Finally, I round out with what I saw at the dairy.

"So, what? You think there's something going on with them?"

"I mean, probably. They've been going to the same small school for a while. I'm sure they have some history. They've just never really mentioned each other. And I'm worried that it has something to do with me."

"Linus, I totally get that, but in reality, they probably have beef that has nothing to do with you. I honestly would try not to worry about it. And, like, don't pry. People tell what they want to tell when they want to tell it."

Olive is one of those people who always presents things in a wise way. Like she's lived way more than thirteen years and knows so much about the world.

"Okay, I'll try to play it cool."

Olive laughs.

Yeah. I don't think I'll be very good at that either.

20
Etta

**WELL, IT LOOKS LIKE INSTEAD OF DIGGING MYSELF *OUT* OF A HOLE,
I JUST GRABBED A SHOVEL AND TRIED TO BURROW STRAIGHT
THROUGH THE CENTER OF THE EARTH . . .**

By the time I make it home, I've missed two calls from Linus. I don't really know what to say to him—other than I hope he decides to run for president. Because my conversation with Marigold went very different than I expected.

For one, despite her innocent **what bet?** text, she seemed to know exactly what I was talking about when we met at Wilcox.

Two, she was pretty insistent that I not back out.

"I don't care," I'd said, definitely louder than I'd had to. And with way bigger arms. "Linus is my friend, and it doesn't feel right to try to get him to do something because you, what? Want him to? That's weird."

Marigold had looked wounded when I said that. Which felt pretty good. But then she doubled down and brought out the big guns.

"You're not the only one who has a relationship with Linus," she said. "Other people can talk to him."

"I know that!" The conversation was exasperating. It felt like we were going in circles. We got louder and louder, and I felt more and more defensive of Linus.

"Fine." She had almost yelled the word. "What if I don't apply to Nova? If Linus is elected president, I won't even submit my application."

"Why would you do that?" I asked, suspicious. I'm still trying to figure it out. What does Marigold have to gain by Linus winning? Why does she care so much?

Honestly, she probably doesn't actually care about Nova and was just saying that she was applying to piss me off. Typical.

Regardless of the reason, it was a really good incentive. Like, a too-good-to-pass-up incentive. Because if Marigold doesn't apply for Nova, that's one more slot that's open for me. So . . . I left Wilcox Dairy not out of the bet like I hoped I would be. But deeper in it.

When I get home, I ask Mom if I can plan a sleepover with Linus for Friday.

"He's a boy," my mom answers. Which isn't an answer.

"Yes. So is Jamie. Can we have a sleepover?" I repeat. I have this sick feeling that Mom might not hold her ground if she knew that Linus was trans. Not that it matters. Not that it makes him less of a boy. Besides, that's not really my information to share.

"I dunno, I would have to . . ."

"Talk to his parents? Fine," I snap. "Call them. See if they're okay with it." I cross my arms and snarl at my mom. I pull out my phone and start texting Linus.

> **Me:** wanna sleepover on Friday? mom is calling ur mom
>
> **Linus:** Sure. But I won't be able to come over until after 7.
>
> **Linus:** Grandma dinner
>
> **Me:** try and stay comfy and stand up for ur self!!!!

I smile at my phone, trying to send good vibes to Linus through the cell signal. Except my throat still feels like crying.

> **Me:** ill plan the perfect horror movie marathon!
>
> **Linus:** ☺

I laugh as I write.

> **Me:** nothing 2 gory
>
> **Me:** ill keep it PG
>
> **Linus:** Is that even possible?
>
> **Me:** it's an expansive genre

I type a question about whether he thinks he'll run for president, but then I delete it.

Linus: What?

Oh, shoot. Caught red-handed. Or text-handed. Ugh, that's terrible. Linus is rubbing off on me.

Me: obsessing over our texts much?
Linus: You're the one typing and deleting!

I swallow and decide to go for it.

Me: just wondering about student council
Linus: like if my first act is going to be adding a
    horror class to the curriculum
Me: first of all: cool
Me: 2 . . .
Linus: . . .
Me: u gonna run?

I close my eyes as I click send. And wait. But no dots show up. No response.

I guess I'll just have to wait in suspense. Which is way worse than any horror movie.

21
Linus

MY MOODY TEENAGER-NESS WAS BOUND TO REAR ITS UGLY HEAD AT SOME POINT.

I spend all of Thursday simultaneously looking for clues about Etta and Marigold's past and trying to pretend that nothing is wrong. The two of them seem as distant as ever. As Friday dinner approaches, I'm on edge when I hear Dad's car pull into the driveway. He picked up Grandma on the way home from work. I'm kind of worried. I might always be worried about these dinners with my grandmother. Because I know she's going to mess up. At some point. My parents have told me again and again that this is hard. For her. For them. Did they forget that this is hard for me?

And then I realize what I'm really worried about. What is secretly freaking me out is that my grandmother might not ever care or think it's worth her time or energy to get my name and pronouns right.

"We're home," Dad calls as he opens the door. Mom

comes out from the kitchen to give Dad a kiss and to hug my grandmother.

"Hi, Mom. Good to see you."

"You saw me on Monday."

"Well, it's good to see you again. And look." She turns and gestures toward me in the living room. "Linus is here!"

"Oh, I thought she might be with her friend again. What was her name? Etta? Lovely name."

I freeze. This isn't a slipup. This is the first thing Grandma is saying about me. And she can't even get it right. I think about what Etta said. About how I can stand up for other people, and I need to do that for myself.

This time, I don't wait and hope that Mom will correct her. I stand up and speak loudly and clearly, like I'm answering questions at the Q&A for student council.

"My name is Linus." My voice sounds different in my ears. Deeper and stronger than it maybe ever has. "I have something to say to you. To all of you." I look at my parents.

Dad does a sort of *Who? Me?* double take.

I swallow and say the next words slowly and deliberately. "My name . . . is Linus."

"Linus," my mom cuts in, her voice thick with warning. I barely get my whole name out. "We've talked about—"

"No, Mom," I say. I'm calm but firm. I'm not yelling.

I'm not throwing a fit. I'm just—I'm just *trying* to explain. To stand up for myself the way Etta told me I can.

"Grandma, since we've moved here I've had dinner with you three times, including tonight, and you've misgendered me on each of those occasions."

"Oh, I had no idea," my grandmother says quietly.

"Well, that's just not good enough. Maybe I should have done a better job of correcting you. But that's . . . that's really, really hard." I start to waver. My voice isn't as strong anymore.

"Okay, Liney, you just correct us, and we'll get it right," Mom says. I can hear her trying to smooth everything over. To move on to dinner-as-planned.

"No," I say. "I mean, yeah, I'll work on that. But you all have to work on it too. It can't just be me who's reminding you." I know they're going to say that they are trying their best. That they just need my help. But I'm thirteen. And I'm tired of being hurt when they get it wrong and even more tired from thinking about whether I should say something about it.

I look at their faces. They look confused and sad. And I don't want them to feel that way, so I keep talking.

"I know it's new for you, Grandma. My name is Linus. I get it. That's hard. I was named after you and you are sentimental about my name."

No. Stop. Stop justifying it. Just—

No! No! This is working. They're listening.

If this mattered to them, they would be getting it right.

My brain fills with thoughts, each straining to be heard over the others. Where I'm normally thinking about hundreds of ways something can go wrong, now I'm thinking of the hundreds of things I should yell. I should scream.

"I'm Linus." My voice comes out hoarse and strained. I sound like a girl. Or not like me.

I wait for a minute, hoping they'll say the right thing. Even though I don't know what that is.

"Maybe we can talk about this over dinner," Mom says, her eyebrows raised.

But the thought of sitting down at the table with my family right now makes my stomach turn, so instead I say, "I'm gonna go sleep over at Etta's," and walk out the door.

——

I run all the way to Etta's house. It's hot out, but I don't care. I'm in a hoodie, but I don't want to stop to take it off. I don't want to look back and make sure my parents aren't following me. I can't do anything but run. I just let my feet hit the pavement over and over. I don't look back.

I'm running away.

In every sense.

My heaving breaths start to drown out the voice in

my head. It's getting quieter the farther I move away from the living room with my confused grandmother and my shocked parents.

Soon, all I can hear is the slap of my shoes. All I can feel is the sweat pooling in the curve of my back. I just go. Go to Etta.

It's probably ten minutes later when Etta opens the door. I'm panting, exhausted from running the ten blocks to her house. She looks confused at first as she pulls out her phone and glances at the time.

"It's five thirty."

"Yeah," I say, slumping over and heaving. Normally, I might be worried that this position makes my boobs more prominent, but Etta already knows I'm trans. Plus, existential crisis and major fight with my family. Who cares about boobs?

Except. I do. Even in this moment of extreme emotion, I'm keenly aware of my body. And the way it isn't what I want.

"So . . . uh . . . dinner got done early . . . ?" Etta stands back, inviting me in.

When I step through the doorway, there's Jamie, Etta's brother. I've met him once before, at dinner. But it's one thing to talk about favorite pizza toppings with someone and another to barge into their house out of breath and basically sobbing.

Etta looks at her brother. "Jamie was just going to

work." She turns to him and jerks her chin in the universal sign for *get lost*.

I wipe my nose, leaving a trail of snot on my hoodie. Gross.

"Yeah, I'm out. Good to see you, Linus." He gives me a wave.

So simple. These people I've known for two weeks can get this right. Why can't my parents?

Tears start streaming down my cheeks.

"Okay, okay!" Etta puts her hand on my shoulder and pulls me into the kitchen where she reaches into the cabinet and pulls out a glass.

In a matter of moments, there's a cold glass of water in my hand. I put it against my mouth and try to drink. Try to focus on each of the muscles I'm using to push the cool liquid down my throat.

Maybe if I can fill my mind with that, I'll forget about my parents.

"Did something happen?" Etta asks quietly, her eyes huge.

"I don't want to talk about it." I finish the water and place the cup in the sink.

"Okay."

Etta shrugs and turns to lead me to the basement. I appreciate that she doesn't push to know more. I'm not even really sure what I would say. My mom didn't stand up for me with my grandmother? I'm upset because, apparently, it's *really hard* to have a trans family member? I think my family might hate me for being trans?

I think back to the way Etta responded when I told her. Like I had told her that my favorite vegetable is broccoli or that I want to be an astronaut. It wasn't that she didn't listen or didn't care. It just didn't seem to throw her. It didn't make me different to her. She just understood more.

The lights in the basement are dimmed and there are purple twinkle lights strung across the ceiling. As we move down the steps, I notice that the whole space is covered in those fake spiderwebs people buy from Target at Halloween. At least I hope they're fake. There are other Halloween decorations strewn about too—a cauldron with green lights making it glow from inside, a skeleton wearing a cowboy hat, and a straight-up haunted-looking doll.

"You did all this for me?" I ask, my eyes huge, as Etta flops down in the middle of a nest of blankets on the floor.

"You wish! We have Halloween 3–6–5 here!" She reaches over to the table next to a ratty brown couch, snags a box of tissues, and chucks it in my direction.

I manage to catch the box and smile. Etta and I are so in sync, we can even play catch—something I never managed to do with any success before. I pull out a tissue and wipe the snot dripping down my face. "That seems excessive."

Etta laughs. "I think you mean *committed*."

"Sure." I playfully roll my eyes and then settle into the nest next to her. "What's on the docket?"

"An eighties classic—*Gremlins*." She produces a DVD box with a picture of a cute little furry thing on it, but it's casting a shadow that looks more sinister.

"Like, these fuzzy Pokémon-looking things?" I say, pointing at the box.

"Unless you break the rules, yes . . . like these fuzzy Pokémon things."

"Okay. That sounds . . . like something I can handle."

Etta grabs the remote to start the movie and hands some Red Vines over to me. My phone chirps. It's Marigold.

Marigold: Hey!! Are you running for prez?

"Shoot!" I mutter under my breath. In all of the running-away-from-home, I completely forgot about student council.

"What?" says Etta, turning to me. "Literally nothing scary has happened yet."

"I just, I have to decide if I'm running for student council president and email Mr. Todd."

"Oh." Etta just says one word, but she looks cagey. Likes she has loads more to say.

"What? You don't have an opinion?"

Etta's clearly biting her tongue. Literally and figuratively.

"Okay . . . so if I say I'm gonna do it . . . you don't care?"

Etta shrugs. But it's the kind of shrug that makes it seems like she might care. I think she cares. She so cares!

"Okay, well . . . I'm gonna email Mr. Todd, then."

"Great . . . ," she says, turning back to the screen. "You're not missing anything important in the movie. JUST THE RULES THAT KEEP THESE LITTLE CUTIES FROM BECOMING KILLING MACHINES."

"Right," I say. I fire off a quick email to Mr. Todd, and then I open my thread with Marigold.

Me: I think so. You?

Marigold: My parents are making me! ☹

Marigold: But I hope you win. You're gonna be so great.

I blush furiously. Good thing Marigold can't see me right now. Covered in snot and beet red.

Me: Thanks.

Marigold: Hey, tomorrow I'm having a party at my house. You should come. You can bring whoever. Open invite.

Me: Cool. I'll try.

Marigold: Things will start around noon.

Marigold: 1908 Piccadilly Cir.

"Who are you texting?" Etta leans over my shoulder. I instinctively tuck my phone into the pocket of my hoodie. I realize I'm hiding this conversation from Etta. After the fight I saw her having with Marigold, I don't really want her to see that I'm texting with Marigold.

"No one."

"Wow. Smooth move, ex-lax!"

"What does that even mean?" I ask.

"How am *I* supposed to know? I'm doomed to repeat the early nineties references of my mother until the end of time."

"Wow. What a curse."

"Totally."

I really appreciate how Etta is just being a friend right now, so I try not to think about my phone and the possible texts that may or may not be coming in from Marigold, and turn my attention to settling in and watching the movie.

22
Etta

GREMLINS RULE #4: DON'T MAKE A BET ABOUT YOUR BEST FRIEND. THAT TURNS YOU INTO A MONSTER.

"This isn't that scary," Linus says when we're about halfway through the movie. The bad gremlins are taking over, but they're more adorable than horrifying. I'm glad he seems calmer. Not that that's saying much. Linus was an absolute wreck when he got here. I tried not to make a big deal about it, but it kind of freaked me out. After the movie got going, I said I had to go to the bathroom and ran up to talk to Mom. I let her know that Linus was in the basement and, in a true out-of-character move, I asked her to call Linus's parents and let them know he's here because I thought they might be worried. Look at me caring about other people's worries!

It's about twenty minutes after that when Mom calls down, "Hey, Mom entering!"

Linus jumps. I grab the remote and pause the movie.

"What's up, Mom?" I ask. I see Linus take a deep

breath next to me and then pull his hood over his head and sink lower into the blanket nest.

"Oh, I'm just checking in on you two."

"Yeah, Linus got here early, so we're getting started," I say. I look at Linus again. He looks like he might feel sick.

"Yeah, I just spoke with Linus's mom." Maybe I'm making it up, but I swear I can feel Linus shudder. "She's worried about you."

"Good." Linus's voice is soft.

I look up at Mom, who definitely heard because she mouths, "What's up?" to me. I shrug. I genuinely don't know. But that lump in my throat seems to be getting worse. Like seeing Linus hurting is hurting me.

"Okay, do you want her to come and get you?" she tries again.

"No!" Linus spins around, looking like he's on the verge of tears again. "I'm fine. Please tell her I'm fine."

"Okay . . . I'm gonna check on you kids in an hour or so." There's some wariness in her voice, but she leaves, and we're able to turn back to the movie.

Linus throws his arms around me.

"Thank goodness I have you," he says, his words muffled against the collar of his sweatshirt. "I mean, moving here has been pretty awful, except I got to meet you. So . . . maybe it's okay."

Honestly, I totally get it. I walked into eighth grade

thinking it would be an absolute drag. The worst year of my life. But then Linus showed up, and suddenly it didn't suck. I started thinking about school in a different way. And I started being happy that I got to spend time with him.

"I'm not so great," I say, leaning into him. "You kind of turned my year around."

"Yeah?" Linus sniffles.

"I mean, I know I give out major stay-away vibes, but that was kind of a new thing for me this year. I had a bad summer."

"Wanna talk about it?" Linus asks.

"Wanna talk about whatever happened to you tonight?"

"Touché."

We snuggle together and watch the rest of *Gremlins*.

I try to swallow the lump in my throat. But it's still there. Telling me I should cry. Or something.

━━━

I spend the rest of the night thinking about three things:

1. I hope that Linus actually likes these movies, and I can work him up to real horror someday.

2. Was Linus serious when he made his comment about running for president?
3. Why won't this crying lump go away?

My phone dings halfway through *Little Shop of Horrors* (how could Linus be scared of a *musical?*). There's a message from Marigold.

Marigold: So you got Linus to run???

I blink. I didn't really *do* anything. Linus is the one who . . .

And then this part of me roars to life. The part of me that wants to crush Marigold Stimpson and be smug about it. The part that wants to make her see what she's missing out on.

Me: Sure did. And he's gonna win too.

I tuck my phone away and hate that the lump in my throat feels worse. Hot and kind of rough. Like maybe I'll throw up.

After we finish *Little Shop*, I ask if Linus is up for something more horror-y.

"I don't really know."

"Come on . . . ," I try to cajole him.

"You said PG. No gore. And I've already done two horror movies."

"Yeah, but those two are, like, *barely* horror movies."

Linus shifts uncomfortably. Is he not having fun? Suddenly, the lump in my throat is made of razor blades and the pit of my stomach drops. I am an absolute trash human. Here I am, forcing Linus to do the thing *I* want to do with no regard for him. And he clearly went through something before coming over.

"Okay, what would *you* like to watch?" I ask. I try to sound light. Inviting. Which I'm sure is at odds with my whole vibe. But with Linus? My vibe takes a new form.

"Can we . . . ," Linus starts. I nod encouragingly. "You're gonna . . ."

I jump in quickly. "I'm not going to laugh or be mad or anything. We can watch whatever you want."

"Can we watch *Easy A*?"

"The rom-com with Emma Stone?" I know what it is. I watched it with Marigold during one of our sleepovers.

Linus smiles ruefully. "Yeah. It's kind of a comfort watch."

"What is comforting about a heteronormative rom-com?!" The words are out of my mouth before I can help it.

Linus smiles. "Stanley Tucci as a father figure." He

shrugs and gives me some primo puppy dog eyes. Linus's secret weapon!

"Fine." I say it in a mockingly reluctant way.

"It really isn't that bad, Etta."

I start searching through the streaming services we've got to find *Easy A*. "I'll be the judge of the merits of Stanley Tucci's performance!"

"He's always a ten, Etta. No debate."

"Fair."

I'm worried that the movie will make me miss my friendship with Marigold, but Linus laughs at all these random lines, so it feels like a completely different experience. And the movie's pretty funny, actually. Not exactly my cup of tea, but not a total snooze-fest. Now that Linus is more comfortable, I can see that I might have made him uncomfortable. Not just with movies, but maybe with other things? Like asking him to run for student council president. And I'm so self-absorbed that I didn't notice.

I have a hard time focusing on the movie. I keep looking over at Linus to see if he's having an okay time. The movie ends with Emma Stone and the hot guy riding on a lawn mower to "Don't You (Forget About Me)," which I know from my mom is referencing a whole bunch of movies from the eighties. It makes me think of that time in civics when I snuck Linus out so he could change his tampon. See, I'm not a *totally* terrible friend!

At least Linus seems calmer. A little more like himself.

✂

The next morning Mom makes her signature sleepover vegan pancakes. Linus has been somber since he woke up. Not even the pancakes seem to be lifting his spirits. Maybe he didn't sleep well. We eat in silence.

Until Linus brings up student council.

"So, I guess I need to come up with a speech. You know, for president."

I try to think of what to say but struggle to find the right words. That lump in my throat is still there and getting in the way. I nod, but inside I'm wondering if this is what Linus really wants.

"I thought you would be excited . . . ?" Linus says, looking wounded.

"I am!" I say a little too quickly. "I just . . ." What do I say? *I don't want to make you do something you don't want to do?* Would that come off as me thinking that I don't think he can do this? *I'm worried that I pushed you into this for the wrong reason?*

"Second batch!" Mom says, setting down a plateful of hot pancakes and saving me from having to come up with something to say. "Etta, is the Nova open house today or tomorrow? I'm trying to coordinate car use with your brother."

The Nova open house! In all the campaigning and crushing Marigold at her own game, I totally forgot!

I pull out my phone and go to the website. The banner pops up. *Join us for an open house on Sunday at noon!*

"It's tomorrow. At noon," I say, my memory amply jogged. Do I need to prepare something? Am I supposed to—

"What's Nova?" Linus asks.

"Oh, it's a school I'm thinking about going to."

"Thinking about?" Mom asks, incredulous. I try to give her a look. You know, one of those looks that says *SHUT. UP.* "Don't let her fool you, Linus. Etta has been dreaming about Nova since she got to Doolittle."

"What's so great about it?" Linus asks.

"Oh, it's . . ." I pause. What *is* so great about Nova? Over the summer, the best part of Nova really seemed like being away from Marigold and regular school. Having space and time to figure things out for myself. Not that regular school has been so bad lately . . . "It's an alternative high school downtown," I finally say. But my voice doesn't sound very excited.

"Oh, so you wouldn't be going to the regular high school?" Maybe I'm imagining it, but Linus seems kind of sad.

"You get a high school diploma. But they work with

you to design a course of study. That's what they call it. I guess the experience is sort of more independent. Gives students more space."

Linus nods. "I can get why that might be appealing."

I think about telling Linus that he should look into it. That we could go there together. But then this awful part of me says I shouldn't. That I'll have enough competition without Linus—who is likable and interesting and about to be student council president if I have anything to say about it. No, better to keep my mouth shut if I want a shot at getting into Nova.

23

Linus

I keep moving my syrup-soaked pancakes around my plate. The last time I had breakfast food like this was that first super early "dinner" at Grandma's when she misgendered me. So, uh, pancakes are great and all, but they aren't exactly giving me warm fuzzies.

I was hoping that the mood would change when I brought up that I was going to run for student council president, but we started talking about that other school instead. Now I'm spiraling thinking about how I found this great friend and we might not even be at the same school next year.

"Oh, Linus, your mom brought that over," Etta's mom says, pointing to my purple duffel bag next to the door.

Mom? She came here? And she just let me be? Should I be mad? Or annoyed that she didn't check on me in person? Or feel good that she cares but isn't pushing? Or . . .

"Oh. Okay, I guess I'll change." Right now I'm wearing some sweats that Etta let me borrow to sleep in. My clothes from yesterday are probably a little ripe, especially since I ran here and then proceeded to repeatedly wipe snot on them, so I definitely don't want to put those on again.

I grab the bag and go into the downstairs bathroom. Mom packed some new underwear, a pair of jeans, and one of my T-shirts. This one is gray and has a picture of a winner's podium with a banner on top that says ROBOT DANCE COMPETITION. The first- and second-place spots are occupied by humans doing the robot dance. The third-place spot has a robot crying on it.

I smile. This shirt always makes me smile.

Mom has also packed some deodorant—thank goodness—a toothbrush, and a hairbrush.

She did not pack a fresh binder.

I took my binder off late last night to sleep. I don't think it's that uncomfortable, but I definitely know when I've worn it for too long. I had wadded it up and put it in the front pocket of my hoodie so I wouldn't lose it. Binders aren't cheap. At least, good ones aren't.

I pull out my mess of a binder and smooth it on the counter of the bathroom. I lean down and smell it. Not great. But not . . . terrible? Hopefully it won't be too much of a problem that I'm wearing the same one again today.

I turn my back to the mirror and peel off my shirt and quickly shimmy into my day-old binder, mashing my breasts up and to the sides until I can look down and almost imagine that they aren't there at all.

Then I pull on the T-shirt and turn back to the mirror.

There. I look like me again.

Chirp.

It's my phone. Pulling me away from my reflection. There are a slew of texts from Mom.

And two from Marigold.

I open Marigold's first.

Marigold: Things are kicking off!

Marigold: Hope you can come!

I smile and look at the time—just after noon. I might still be able to make it to the party.

My thumb hovers over the word *Mom* on my phone. I suck in a deep breath and click over to her texts. They're all from last night.

Mom: Just checking in . . .

Mom: I dropped off an overnight bag at Etta's.

Mom: Please call.

I take another deep breath. My mind is going a million miles a minute imagining all the ways the call can go. Very few of them feel particularly good. Actually, none of them seem good. That realization causes my heart to beat faster. Like it's rushing to catch up with my brain.

I take a deep breath and call.

"Sweetie—Linus—I'm so glad you called."

"Yeah. Thanks for bringing me my clothes," I say. I don't mention that she forgot a binder.

"Do you want me to come pick you up?" This is weird. I thought Mom was going to yell at me. Or demand that I come home right away so we can talk about how inappropriate my behavior was. Or a thousand other *ors*, all of them equally dire.

I wasn't expecting *this*.

"Uh, I'm hoping to go to a party-thing at Marigold's," I say.

"Who's Marigold?" Mom asks.

"She's a girl from school." *That I have a huge crush on*, I silently tack on.

"I can give you a ride," Mom responds. Wow, that was easy. Maybe I should run away from home more often? "Is Etta going?"

Um, I don't know. *Is* Etta going? She's been acting weird. Or maybe *I've* been acting weird. And maybe she just needs a change of scene. I guess I could invite her?

"I'll check," I say. I kind of hope Etta *does* come so I don't have to brave the car ride alone with Mom. Not yet.

"I'll be there in ten minutes, okay?"

"Okay." I hang up the phone and move to put on the rest of my clothes.

When I get out of the bathroom, Etta looks at my shirt for about fifteen seconds and then busts out laughing.

"That's a great one!" she says. I join her in laughing. It feels good. Way better than panicking.

"Hey, my mom is picking me up to go to an eighth-grade party. Do you want to come?"

Etta's eyes dart away. She doesn't want to come. She doesn't have to say it. I just know. And that's okay. I try to believe that.

"Etta, you should go!" her mom pipes in. "You don't have any plans today, since the Nova open house is tomorrow."

Etta looks at me, and I give her what I hope is a very good set of puppy dog eyes.

She finally caves. "How can I say no to that face?"

When Mom drives up, Etta and I are back to easygoing. Joking about how we can save each other from awkward situations at the party. The car ride is jovial. Simple. Nice.

Until we pull into 1908 Piccadilly Circle.

That's when Etta freaks.

24
Etta

THE ONE PLACE I ABSOLUTELY DO NOT WANT TO BE ON A SATURDAY AFTERNOON IS AT A POOL PARTY AT MY EX-BEST FRIEND'S HOUSE.

We're at Marigold's.

How did I not ask Linus about where we were going? How did he not know there would be ZERO chance of me going to this party had I known about the Marigold of it all, puppy dog eyes notwithstanding?

I don't know how I didn't realize we were heading here sooner.

Maybe it was that things felt right with Linus after a night of them feeling . . . not so right.

I freeze, staying in my seat and wondering how weird it would be to ask Ms. Stout to drive me back home. I mean . . . it would be pretty weird. But wouldn't it be worth it? To not set foot in Marigold's territory?

"You coming?" Linus sounds happy. Like he has no clue that I'm 1000 percent not coming at all.

"Oh, I . . . I just realized . . ." What? What did I

realize? That I have something to do? Even though my mom LITERALLY SAID THAT I HAVE NO PLANS TODAY?! MOM, WHY COULDN'T YOU JUST LET ME—

"This might be a good opportunity to campaign for president," Linus says, smiling at me. My guilt creeps back into my throat. If I felt sick at the mere thought of being at Marigold's, Linus's mention of the campaign makes me want to double over. But then he simply says, "Come on. We'll stick together." Linus holds his hand out to me. He doesn't give me puppy dog eyes. This look is something else. Something more genuine. More kind. More quintessentially Linus.

And even though I'm still not sure, I take Linus's hand and let him pull me out of the car.

"Text when you're ready to come home, okay?" Linus's mom calls out.

Linus nods, but his mouth falls into a straight line. Like he isn't sure if he can smile at her.

We walk up to the door, but there is a sign taped to it: 8TH GRADE PARTY OUT BACK!

Marigold's backyard looks the same as it did last year. Like any normal middle schooler's dream spot for a party. There's an upper deck, and beyond that, there's a pool and a small pool house. I remember thinking that Marigold's house was so amazing when we first became friends. I mean . . . who has a pool in Ohio, a state where the weather is literally disgusting nine months out of the year?

Now it just feels like so much.

And there is one major difference between Marigold's house when I used to visit and Marigold's house now.

When I used to visit, it would just be the two of us bobbing in the pool for hours on end. Now it looks as though the whole eighth grade is here.

Everyone was invited.

Everyone except me.

I'm only here because Linus invited me. Not because I was actually included.

Even Linus, the new kid, managed to get an invite above me.

I mean. I don't care. Why would I care?

At least, that's what I try to tell myself.

Besides, it's probably a good thing that everyone else is here. Really. With so many guests, I might be able to avoid Marigold altogether.

Linus and I make our way through the crowd. A group of boys badger Linus to jump into the pool with them. Linus waves them off and looks at me desperately. I know it's not just the fact that we don't have swim-suits that has him declining. Etta to the rescue! I run over and grab his hand, saying, "I NEED TO TALK TO YOU RIGHT NOW!!" Linus shrugs at the boys, who quickly move to taking off their shirts and sprinting for the water. Linus laughs and follows me behind the pool house.

"Close one!" he whispers at me, a bright smile pasted on his face as we hear a bunch of girls screaming as they're splashed by the swimmers. "Thanks for saving me from death by pool!"

"No problem. That's what friends are for!" I smile back at him, but my smile falters when hushed voices catch my ear. At first, I just hear the S sounds, but I creep a little closer to the source. So does Linus.

"—pretty sure this whole party is just a ploy to get votes . . ."

There is a voice coming from around the other corner of the pool house.

"Honestly, that's kind of pathetic."

"For sure."

I'm not sure who's talking, but I'm pretty sure I know *who* they are talking about. And . . . in this weird moment, I feel bad for Marigold. Sure, I think she's terrible and awful and whatever, but that's because she did something terrible and awful to me. What did she do to these people? Invite them to a party? Wow, what a monster. I'm almost about to run out and say something, when I notice Linus is already on the move.

He stumbles around the corner, though I'm pretty sure there's nothing in Marigold's pristine backyard for him to slip on.

"Oh, sorry!" I hear him say. "I was just looking for the bathroom?"

"Oh, um . . ."

"And I really hope you weren't suggesting that Marigold is trying to buy your votes for president. Earlier. Sorry, couldn't help but overhear. You were kind of . . . loud."

"What? Oh . . . Uh . . ."

"The bathroom?" I have to admire Linus's ability to deploy passive-aggression like a weapon of mass destruction.

"Oh, it's in the pool house . . ."

"And we weren't saying that—"

"Oh, sure. I mean, it just sounded that way. Just be careful about what you say. People might take things out of context."

Wow. I don't know that I expected Linus to be such a passive-aggressive assassin, but I'm impressed by his ability to shut down that conversation. Even if I can't help but agree with some of what those girls were saying. I hear steps and a door open as he goes into the pool house to pretend to use the bathroom.

All alone, I circle back to the pool.

I must look ridiculous. We're at a pool party, and here I am in my all-black getup with heavy eyeliner and green hair. I've never really minded when I look out of place before, but something about this moment makes me feel particularly . . . vulnerable. Like I'm exposing myself in some weird way. I wait for another minute, hoping that Linus will come back from the bathroom soon and rescue me.

He doesn't come.

So I go to the pool house, open the door . . . and there he is.

Kissing Marigold.

What?

The?

Hell?

25

Linus

FOR ABOUT TEN SECONDS, THINGS WERE ACTUALLY *GOOD*?
UNTIL THEY BECAME TERRIBLE. WITH SPECIAL SAUCE!

When I go into the pool house, I'm not expecting someone to already be in here.

But someone is.

It's Marigold.

And she's crying.

"Oh, hi . . . Marigold."

"Hey, Linus." The way she says it makes it seem like it might be okay that I'm in here with her. So I tentatively move in her direction. She's sitting on the floor, looking miserable. I think about how Etta gave me a glass of water when I came to her house, crying and broken. I look around and can't find a cup. Or a sink. So I settle for the next best thing—or, in this case, the only thing—a towel. I grab one from one of the racks against the walls of the pool house and hand it to her. Marigold looks at me and sniffles before taking the towel and burying her face in it. She lets out a muffled scream. I look away. This seems like a private thing.

"Thanks," she mutters against the towel.

I turn back. "I guess you overheard stuff," I say, squatting down next to her.

"I heard . . . everything." She looks at me, her eyes shining with tears. "Thanks for . . . saying what you said."

"Oh, that? It was . . ."

"It wasn't nothing. You didn't have to say anything. You did. It's something. It's everything."

I blush. Like MAJORLY. I mean, I'm always blushing around Marigold, but this is next-level.

"Look, Linus. I . . . I really like you. Like, a lot." Is *she* blushing? WHAT IS HAPPENING?! My eyes feel like they've grown huge. Unblinking in shock and wonder. "And I really, really hope that you can get past that . . . that I tried to get to know you through that bet."

I blink. "What?"

"You know . . . Etta and I made that ridiculous bet that she . . . that she could get you elected student council president."

Etta and Marigold made a . . . a bet?

"What are you talking about?"

Understanding blooms across Marigold's face. I'm still in the dark though. What is she talking about? "I . . . I liked you. And I wanted to spend more time with you.

So I dared Etta that she couldn't get you elected to student council president."

Marigold likes me. I want to spend a moment focusing on that. But I can't. Because this isn't just about Marigold liking me. It's about Etta too. "What did she get out of it?"

Marigold shrugs. But my mind starts racing. Thinking about everything that Etta and I have been through. Everything we've done over the past two weeks. Was that all—

"I don't believe you," I say, cutting off my own thoughts. "Etta is my friend, she wouldn't—" I sputter, stringing together flimsy reasons why Etta couldn't possibly be my friend because of a bet.

As I'm babbling, Marigold pulls out her phone and holds up the screen. There are texts. Between her and Etta.

> **Etta:** Hey, M. I think we need to talk about the bet.
>
> Can you meet at Wilcox Dairy in ten?
>
> **Me:** What bet?
>
> **Me:** the Linus on student council thing?
>
> **Me:** sure
>
> **Me:** So you got Linus to run???
>
> **Etta:** Sure did. And he's gonna win too.

I stop reading. Not that there's anything else to read. It's enough. It's too much.

"Why would she . . . ?"

Marigold tucks her phone away. "I mean, I'm kind of glad she did it. For whatever reason. Because now . . . now . . . we're . . ." Marigold puts her hand on my cheek, and I get impossibly hotter. "Now we know each other. And . . . we like . . . each other?" She says the last bit like it's a question. I mean, she's already said that she likes me, so I guess she's asking if I like her. Which . . .

"Of course, but—"

"Oh, good!"

And then she's bringing her mouth to brush against mine, and I sit there for a minute and let her. It's . . . not totally mind-blowing. I mean, I've watched enough rom-coms to have really worked up how great my first kiss is going to be. But it's pretty nice, all things considered. Not that I know so much about kissing. I mean, the fact that my first kiss is with my crush. Wow, that's pretty great! Am I thinking too much? Should I be doing something? I try to pay attention to what Marigold is doing. But she's just pressing her mouth to mine.

How do I breathe again?

For a minute, I panic and wonder if the choice is: Stop kissing Marigold Stimpson or Death? Neither of which sound particularly appealing.

But just as I am about to turn blue, I remember that my nose exists, so I take a clumsy pull through my nostrils and let Marigold sit there. Her mouth against mine.

And then the door opens.

Marigold pulls away from me, so I do the same. And then I look to the doorway. It's Etta. Her face looks disgusted? Horrified? Disappointed?

I think about that phrase that parents say. "I'm not mad, I'm just disappointed." That's Etta right now.

"What are you—what are you doing?" She can barely get the words out. Okaaaaaay, scratch that. She's mad. Really, really, really mad.

Maybe it's because she is so mad and indignant, but suddenly, I get mad and indignant back.

"I was kissing Marigold," I say, my voice quiet. "I can make up my own mind about things."

"What are you talking about? How could you kiss—" Etta sputters and points at Marigold in horror.

"Stop. I already stood up for her once. I'll do it again." This voice doesn't feel like mine. And the words taste weird in my mouth, but I can't seem to stop. Because for all I know, I mean nothing to Etta. I'm just a way for her to prove something to Marigold.

"You'll stand up for her against me? *I'm* your friend!" Etta's voice is high, her eyes wide.

The word *friend* crashes against my ears. Because based on what Marigold just told me, that's not true.

"Are you?" My words are icy, trying to hurt Etta the way she's hurting me.

"Yes! Of course!" Etta screams.

I pause and lean in. This is my chance to see if what Marigold said is true. "I thought I was just a bet." I say the words close to Etta's face, staring her straight in the eyes to make sure I catch her reaction.

Etta gasps, but she doesn't deny it. My heart crackles. Before this, pain was just a possibility, but now it's real. And horrible. Etta walks out of the doorway, but I follow her. Suffering and furious.

"Tell me the truth! Why did you . . . why did you first start hanging out with me?" I yell as I chase her down.

Etta keeps walking away.

"Etta. Stop."

"No, Linus. I'm not having this conversation right now." She keeps walking, like she knows exactly where she's going.

"Well, I am!" I'm screaming now. I plant my feet and cross my arms.

Etta spins around. "Fine. FINE! *She*—" She points at Marigold, who is standing in the doorway of the pool house. "*She* has been a monster to me for months. I told you. I told you about my friend who ruined everything. It's *her*, Linus. And I saw a chance to get back at her. I didn't make the bet. *She* did. Before I even *knew* you. She dared me and said I couldn't get you elected."

"So . . . it's true." There's new heartbreak here. Because even though I saw the recognition in her eyes, a part of me was hoping that she would deny it. Even if it was true. Or explain that I was misunderstanding the situation. But I wasn't. Etta became my friend because of a bet. I'm not likable. I'm not interesting. I'm not worth getting to know.

Etta only believed in me because she wanted to get back at someone else. Not because of me. Not because of us.

Suddenly, I notice how quiet it is. The boys in the pool aren't splashing; the mean girls aren't bad-mouthing Marigold; the music isn't playing. Everyone is just staring at Linus, the loser who can't make his own friends.

"Linus, but then, then, I got to know you . . . and it wasn't about . . ." Etta's voice is quiet. She trails off, looking around at everyone staring at her. Her words dry up. She can't pretend in front of a crowd.

"Find your own ride home," I say. I'm out.

I walk out of the backyard and to the driveway, where I sit on a decorative boulder next to Marigold's mailbox. I wait for someone to follow me. To see how I am. Marigold. Etta. A random eighth grader.

But no one comes.

So I pull my knees up to my chest and cry until Mom comes and gets me.

26
Etta

**DESPERATE TIMES AND MAJOR SCREWUPS CALL FOR GRAND
ROM-COM-INSPIRED (YET DEEPLY PLATONIC) GESTURES.**

I call Linus fifty-two times over the next twenty-two hours.

I text him eighty-four times.

He never answers.

I check that I have my phone roughly twenty times as Mom drives me to the Nova open house. Nothing.

I keep my notifications on and my sound turned up . . . just in case. Because if he calls, I need to . . . I need to be there. I need to explain.

At the beginning of the Nova open house, the principal gives a big talk about how we should turn off our cell phones and be in this moment . . . that there is no call that could be more important than our futures. I rolled my eyes. I didn't expect Nova would make me roll my eyes so soon.

My phone chirps about ten minutes into the opening presentation. I pull it out right away, and everyone around me gives me the side-eye. I don't care. What if it's Linus?

It isn't. It's Mom texting to let me know that Jamie is on pickup duty.

I put my phone away and turn back to the presentation.

There's a different adult talking now . . . describing how students at Nova work with an academic adviser to design, revise, and execute an individualized course of study.

"Of course, we need to make sure you have the basics down! We meet all the state requirements, so no worries there, parents." There are a few chuckles from parents in the audience. I start to wonder how different Nova really is from . . . other schools.

I sit through the rest of the presentation, and even though I still like the idea of Nova, my burning *need* to get here as soon as possible is . . . not as strong. After the presentation, students are invited to talk with an admissions counselor. I wait my turn, anxiously checking my phone for any signs of Linus. Even if just those three dots would appear, I would know that he's seen my texts. That he's thinking about me. Thinking about responding. And that's something.

It's finally my turn to go into the admissions office.

A woman with long brown hair and huge glasses waves me in. She doesn't smile, just gestures that I should take a seat.

"Hello . . ." She draws out the word like she's waiting for me to fill in the rest of the greeting.

"Oh, Etta. I'm Etta."

"And I'm Ms. Stark." I wait for her to say that it's nice to meet me. She doesn't. I guess it's not nice to meet me. "What classes are you taking at your current school?" She's looking at her laptop as she speaks.

"Oh, the normal ones, I guess."

"Grade-level academics. Any particular points of high performance or stress?"

"Um . . ." The only thing I can think of is that I'm not very good at math. I guess that might be considered a point of stress or whatever. But that doesn't seem like the thing to tell an admissions counselor. "Not really."

"And extracurriculars . . ."

I take a breath. "I'm the campaign manager for my friend who just got elected to student council. And now we are working to get him elected president."

I expect her to ask questions about student council. To perk up a little. But she doesn't. Instead, she just says, "Anything else?"

"Um . . . I . . ." I had really been planning to talk more about the student council thing. "I like horror movies?" I squeak.

"Did you start a club or something?" Her voice is monotone.

"No, I just watch them with my friend."

Ms. Stark looks up at me and closes her laptop. "Okay. Etta, was it?" I nod. "I'm going to be honest. Nova is in high demand at the moment. That means we are looking at a very competitive pool of applicants."

I nod.

"So you just want to think carefully about whether Nova is something you really want to go for. And how you will feel if you get in. And how you will feel if you don't get in."

I nod again. I appreciate that she's talking to me and not looking at her computer. Not feeding me some line. She seems to really be telling me something important. I lean in.

"I just urge you to make sure that you really want—"

And then my phone rings. Full blast *Exorcist* theme filling this poor woman's office.

"Sorry!" I say. I pull it out, and a picture of Linus making a ridiculous face flashes on the screen. I look at Ms. Stark. And I look back at my phone.

"My time is very limited, Etta."

"I totally get that, but I—"

"And I believe Mr. Tucker made our feelings about phones pretty clear in his presentation at the beginning of the open house."

"Yeah, it's just . . ." I look back at my phone again. How many rings have there been? Five? Am I going to miss Linus's call?

"Etta, if going to Nova is a priority, make it a priority. If it isn't . . . don't waste your or my time. Think about what you really want."

My phone stops ringing. I stare at it, praying that Linus will leave a voice mail.

"Are you going to silence your phone?" Ms. Stark asks.

I look at her. And I think about what I really want.

And the answer is: I'm not sure.

"I'm thirteen," I say. "I don't think . . . I don't know what I really want. I don't think it's a waste of anyone's time for me to apply to Nova. I think it could be . . . it could be a great experience. But . . ." I look at my phone. No voice mail notification. "But someone I really care about is hurting, and I . . . That's taking my attention right now. I'm sorry. I'll let you talk to other students who are ready to be fully present."

I stand up. Maybe I'm just a kid and maybe I don't know how to make priorities, but I know I want to do whatever I can to make Linus stop hurting. And if he's willing to let me help, then I need to be there for him. As I'm walking, I call Linus. He doesn't answer. But he called. That must mean something.

—

I get to Linus's house on foot and knock on his door. As I wait, I text Jamie to let him know where I am for pickup, and then I scroll through my phone to pull up Spotify so I can play "Don't You (Forget About Me)." I'm doing it because of *Easy A*, which did it because of *The Breakfast Club*. I'm a cliché of a cliché of a cliché. And I don't give a crap.

The song plays, and Linus's mom comes to the door. I pause my phone.

"Is Linus home? I really need to talk to him. To . . . apologize."

"I'll see."

So . . . he's home. He just might not come and see me.

So, that's a terrible proposition.

I wait. Then I press play, hoping to lure Linus out with eighties pop music and a quasi-grand gesture.

I wait more.

I hope he comes.

I text him.

Me: please come out. I need to apologize.

I wait.

I wait.

And then there are steps. Are they Ms. Stout's? Or Linus's?

And then he's there. Standing on the other side of the screen door. He isn't smiling. He looks tired and has his arms crossed over his chest.

I hold my phone over my head, like I'm blasting a boom box in one of those rom-coms that he likes. Sure, I haven't seen the original movie, but I can hang with a reference.

Linus doesn't smile.

I bring my phone down.

"Linus. I'm . . . I'm so glad you came to talk to me."

No response.

"Or at least to listen." I take a breath. The music is still playing. I fumble with my phone . . . this apology doesn't really work with a soundtrack. "Okay, so . . . I wanted to explain. Well, first I want to apologize. Because I know I hurt you. And that was never what I wanted. Especially now. Because . . . you . . . you're, like, really important to me."

I take another breath. This one makes my whole body shake when I let it out.

"Marigold was my best friend. For years and years. And then . . . last summer. She just . . . stopped. I told you about that. When we were texting. I don't really know why she didn't want to hang out with me. All I know is that it hurt. It hurt so much. And . . . when she . . . okay, sorry, I'm getting ahead of myself. That day of the assembly when Mr. Todd announced the elections for student council, I made a comment about the students at Doolittle being puppets and doing whatever was popular. And . . . Marigold heard me. And . . . I don't really remember how we got to making the bet, but we did. And she named you as the person. She bet that I couldn't get you elected. And I was . . . I was still hurting. And I just wanted to win. I wanted to beat her. And maybe make her hurt. So I accepted.

"I know that the reason all of this started isn't good. But I'm glad that it made me get to know you. Even if it was for a not-good reason at first."

I look at him. I can't really tell what Linus's expression is through the screen of his front door.

"So I'm asking you to forgive me. And maybe . . . maybe we can figure out what it is *you* want. If you want to be on student council or visit the petting farm every weekend or watch rom-coms eternally. I'll do whatever you want. Please. I'm . . . I'm so sorry."

Then Linus pushes open the door. This is it. We're going to hug. We're going to cry. We're going to do everything you do when you make up with your best friend after a surely-meaningless-in-the-long-run fight.

Right?

Instead, Linus hands me a piece of paper that's folded in half.

I NEED MORE TIME.

That's what's scrawled on the front of it.

"Of course," I say. Because what else do you say

when you've destroyed trust with your best friend and would do anything just to get them to forgive you? You do exactly what he asks you to do.

Linus steps back into the doorway and crosses his arms again.

As I'm walking away toward Jamie's car, I unfold the paper.

And there is the list we made. On the way to the haunted barn. I read through all the great things.

THINGS ABOUT LINUS
CARES ABOUT OTHER PEOPLE
GOOD SENSE OF HUMOR
MOM HAS A GOOD SENSE OF HUMOR
FRESH PERSPECTIVE ABOUT DOOLITTLE
EASY TO TALK TO
GOOD SMILE
GOOD HEART

And then I notice there is another list. And it's . . . it's about me. From Linus.

THINGS ABOUT ETTA
PROTECTIVE OF FRIENDS (LIKE A WOLF)
GETS JOKES (EVEN IF SHE DOESN'T LAUGH) = SMART!
ALWAYS WILLING TO COMMIT TO A BIT (SEE THING
ABOUT MY MOM BEING FUNNY)

KNOWS A LOT ABOUT DOOLITTLE
FUN TO TALK TO
SUPERCOOL DAGGER GLARE
GOOD HEART

As we drive away from Linus's house, I start to cry. When did Linus write this? And more important, does he still believe any of it?

27
Linus

VOTE LINUS STOUT AND MAKE SPACE FOR CHANGE!
(NOW, *THAT'S* A SLOGAN!)

Some days feel longer than others. But from the moment after my fight with Etta to me sitting backstage at the Doolittle auditorium feels like no time at all. Even though a lot happens.

For one, after Mom picked me up, I had my big hash out with Mom and Dad.

"Can we talk?" I asked both of them when I walked through the door.

"Sure. Of course, Linus." I noticed Mom used my name. I wondered if she noticed too.

"I want to talk about what happened with Grandma. The first time and, well, all of it."

Mom nodded. It was almost like she was nervous. Which was weird. Because . . . do parents get nervous?

"It didn't feel good."

"It didn't feel good to me either," Mom said.

"I get that. I mean, I get that you want me to be

patient. But this is who I am. I don't want to be patient anymore. And it hurts me when *you're* patient. Like you care about Grandma's comfort more than you care about mine. And my identity."

I watched as tears started streaming down Mom's face. Dad leaned over to squeeze Mom's shoulder. I waited for a minute, thinking that might be the moment for them to chime in. But after ten Mississippis, I spoke again.

"So . . . I'm . . . I guess I'm asking you to stand up for me."

"You shouldn't have to ask." She was really crying at that point. Hard. I was too.

"Well, I'm asking. I've been asking."

"I'm sorry, Linus. I'm . . . I know I mess up a lot."

I didn't say it was okay. It isn't. And not lying about it was a way I could stand up for myself. But I went and wrapped Mom in a hug. Dad joined too.

When I pulled away, she kept her hands holding the sides of my arms, and Dad had his hand on my shoulder. "But I know better. I'm going to ask more. About you. About what you need. And I'm going to do better."

"Did you know I'm running for student council president?" I asked.

"I knew you were on the student council . . . I didn't . . . No. I didn't know." She started crying again then. But this time she was smiling a little.

"Well, I am. And when I was working with Etta, a big

thing we talked about was making space for people to feel comfortable at school. I want to feel comfortable at home. And at Grandma's. I want you to feel comfortable too."

"I hope that's possible."

"I just . . . I just don't believe that our comfort is incompatible."

"You're a pretty smart kid."

"Nah," I said, even though I secretly thought she might be right. "I've just . . . been thinking about this a lot. Anyway, I would really like you both and Grandma to come see my speech. It's Monday morning at school. First thing. I just think . . . maybe it will help for her to see me being myself." I shrugged then.

"Honey, that's so thoughtful. And brave. It's brave too."

Maybe it is. I don't know.

Then there was Etta's apology. Mom told me that I didn't have to go and talk to her. And I didn't exactly talk to her. I needed time. So I told her that.

But I also gave her that list.

Because there's this part of me that hopes beyond hope that it wasn't just a bet. That the things she thought about me and wrote on that list are things she really believes. I know I really believe what I wrote about her.

I also texted Marigold. I told her we needed to talk in person, that there was too much to say. We agreed to both get to school early and meet backstage, just before we go head-to-head for student council president.

I spent the night thinking about all of it: my parents, Etta, Marigold, the election. And, as the night wore on, it became clearer and clearer that what I really wanted was my friend back.

I thought about texting Etta. But I didn't. Because even though I want Etta back in my life, I need to do this for myself.

I need to see if this is what I want.

"Hey, Linus," Marigold says. It's the first time we've talked since the kiss, and if I thought I was awkward around Marigold before, I've managed to unlock a whole new level by kissing her.

"Hey." As Etta's mom would say: Smooth move, ex-lax.

"Look, everything got really messed up."

"That sounds like an understatement," I agree. "I talked to Etta. Or, I heard what she had to say about all of this."

"Oh." Marigold hangs her head.

"I don't really want to get into being some kind of trophy for you to lord over each other—"

"That's not what you are!"

I hold up a hand. Because the conversation I need to have with Marigold isn't about Etta. "And I also don't want to be a go-between. You two clearly have history. Whether you want to figure it out is up to you."

"I get that," she concedes.

"I know that boys in middle school are monumentally terrible at talking about their feelings, but I actually did like you," I say.

"Did?"

"Did." Her eyes dart away nervously. "And maybe could. We're always changing. Always figuring out new things."

"The kiss was that bad?" she asks, a small smile on her lips like she knows her kiss was anything but bad. "We can't even be friends?"

"Right now, we're just two eighth graders running for student council president. After that, we'll see." I hold out my hand, and she returns the gesture. And even though I know she was kind of mean to Etta and made a bet that brought about some pretty terrible emotions for me, I still get that zip up my arm. A zip that says liking Marigold is still very much a possibility.

✄

Everything is ready. And I'm still nervous. For a million different reasons. For Grandma. For Etta. For Marigold. For the rest of the school.

And I'm also sure.

It's strange. But I can be both at once.

Nervous and sure.

I'm standing backstage. Marigold's speech is muffled because the backstage speaker doesn't seem to be working properly. But when her speech ends, there's a huge cheer. Which is my cue. I'm next.

I poke my head out from behind the curtain and hear Mr. Todd say, "Next up, we have Linus Stout."

I take a breath, walk out, and wait. Everything is quiet, and then I pull up "Don't You (Forget About Me)" on my phone, put up the volume as loud as it will go, and hold it over my head as I make my way to the podium. I shade my eyes and look out into the audience.

And there's Etta. Sitting in the front row. In her Etta finest. Black clothes. Green hair. Except tears are streaming down her face. I can tell because her eyeliner is running down her face with them. I give her a little wave. She waves back. Then I wave to the crowd, even though I can't really see much through the lights.

"Hello! I'm Linus Stout, and I'm running for student council president." My voice echoes out into the crowd.

"You might be wondering who I am. Which is fair. Because I'm new to the school, and I haven't met most of you. Well, if you're in the eighth grade you might know me—from running for student council or for having the fight heard round the world at that pool party this weekend." There are a few laughs at that.

"So, hi! I'm Linus. And . . ." I swallow. "My pronouns are he/him/his." I pause. "But those aren't the pronouns I've always used. I'm trans. And . . . I just . . . It's a part of who I am. So, I wanted to share that with you."

It's absolutely silent. You could hear a pin drop. I think back to when I first arrived at Doolittle and how my plan was to lay low. It took two weeks for me to buck that idea entirely. I sit in the silence and wait for my brain to think of the hundreds of ways this will go wrong, but instead . . . I just look out and see Etta. She lifts her arms and wraps them around herself, giving me a hug across time and space.

I take a breath and keep going. "The thing is, all of us are going through huge changes—transitions—during our middle school years. Maybe you were a soccer star, but now you want to try out for the play. Maybe your parents are getting divorced, and life at home is very different. Our lives change. And our understandings of ourselves change. And . . . I just want to make space. For you—for *us*—to figure out what *we* want." I look at Etta when I say that line. Because she said it to me on the porch. "And what we want can change. Let's make space for those changes. In ourselves, in our friends, and in our school. So if you are looking to make space for change, vote for Linus."

There's applause. It's hard to tell if it's a lot or a

normal amount. Or maybe less than normal. Or if it's boisterous or polite. I don't really care because Etta leaps out of her seat and wraps me in an in-the-spotlight hug. Onstage. In front of everyone.

No one is too cool for a best friend.

—

As the auditorium starts to clear out, Mom walks up with Grandma and Dad.

"Hi, Grandma," I say.

"Hello, Linus." I think that's going to be it, but then she says, "That was very impressive. I'm proud to call you my grandson."

I smile and nod at her. We still have a ways to go, but this is something. And we can keep making space.

Etta is standing next to me as I wave my parents away.

"I know, I know. You don't want us standing around and embarrassing you," Mom says.

"Exactly," I say solemnly. "It's part of my duty as a newly minted teen to shun my parents. Shun! Shun!"

I turn to Etta, who gives me our hand signal, and we both dissolve into a fit of giggles. After the giggles fade, Etta turns to me, serious.

"I'm sorry."

"I know."

"Okay. I just . . . I'll keep saying it if I have to." She throws her arms around me and hugs me again.

"I'm sure we'll both mess up in the future."

"For sure."

"For now, though, I need help getting to civics class."

Etta smiles. "We're going to the same place." She reaches her hand toward mine, and I take it. "Follow me."

28
Etta

AT THE END OF *CARRIE*, CARRIE'S ARM SHOOTS UP FROM THE GRAVE TO GRAB SOMEONE. AT THE END OF THIS STORY, YOU GET HALLOWEEN COSTUMES. BUT, LIKE, THEY'RE *GREAT* HALLOWEEN COSTUMES.

"You almost ready?" I ask.

"Almost. It's more complicated than I thought," Linus's voice shouts out from the school bathroom. Somehow, he convinced me to help with decorations for the Doolittle Middle Halloween Party. I mean, I doubt there's anyone with more impeccable Halloween taste than me . . . but still!

"All right. Here we go," Linus shouts. Then he comes running out of the bathroom. "Ta-da!"

He's dressed in black sweats, and pinned all over him are those tiny cereal boxes. Each one has a tiny knife in it with red "blood" running down the box. Cap'n Crunch; Snap, Crackle, and Pop; Tony the Tiger—they're all slain.

"I'm a . . . CEREAL KILLER." Linus makes finger guns and points them toward me.

I look at him for another second and then bust out laughing.

Then I hold up my hand and wiggle it.

"A laugh *and* a hand signal. Wow. I think my work here is done." Linus brushes his hands together, looking smug and delighted.

"Hardly," I say. "We still have a middle school party to run, Mr. President."

The election was close, but in the end, Linus pulled it out. I expected to feel more smug about Linus winning, particularly since he beat out Marigold. But in the end, the fact that he won had very little to do with me. Since the announcement of the results, I've talked to Marigold a few times, once to tell her that she could apply to Nova if she really wanted to. Linus convinced me that part of purging the bad vibes of the bet included voiding the results.

Linus's reign has been in effect for a little over a month, and he's been doing a bang-up job. Even I, the resident anti-lots-of-things girl, think so.

"Are you sure you want to stay?" Linus says. "I know your application is due."

He's right. My application for Nova is due tomorrow. November first. And I filled it out. I was thoughtful. But obsessing over it now won't do anything.

Besides, I'm not even sure if that's what I want anymore.

A wise person once said that what we want can change.

"Nah. I've got to show you *my* costume," I say. Then I make my way into the bathroom and pull on my own garment.

I emerge from the bathroom in my greatest creation to date. A re-creation of Belle's yellow dress from *Beauty and the Beast* adorned with tacos and the necessary fixings. My green hair is complemented with bits of felt lettuce.

When I pop out, Linus just stares at me.

"Um . . . do you get it? I'm . . ."

"TACO BELLE!" Linus runs up and hugs me while laughing wildly. I feel some of his cereal boxes crush against my costume.

"Whoa, be careful!"

"They're already dead!" he says, throwing up his hands in the most enthusiastic *that's hilarious* sign I've ever seen. "I can't believe you did a pun costume!" Linus cheers.

"I can't believe you did a horror-movie-pun costume!"

"We're growing on each other!"

"Soon you'll have green hair!"

Linus laughs.

"That's not a no!"

"Maybe we'll start with blue," he says.

"Whatever you want."

"It doesn't need to be whatever I want. It can be whatever we want!"

I smile at Linus and he smiles at me. Just a cereal killer and a Taco Belle. Two best friends. Who are weird and happy.

━

ACKNOWLEDGMENTS

Thank you to everyone who works to get trans books into the world—particularly those who get these stories into the hands of young people. For *Linus and Etta Could Use a Win*, that includes . . .

You! Maybe you read *Skating on Mars* and are a Caroline Huntoon devotee (aka my parents). Maybe you picked up *Linus and Etta Could Use a Win* because the cover caught your eye. Maybe someone handed you this book and said, "Here. Read this." Whatever your path to meeting Linus and Etta, thank you for following it and for supporting this story.

My writing friends—Jamie Rubenstein, Edward Underhill, Jen St. Jude, Justine Pucella Winans, Ronnie Riley, and Kate Fussner—who repeatedly reminded me that getting one book out in the world was not a total fluke and getting another out was definitely within my capabilities. I look forward to that continual stream of reassurance for as long as I am a writer.

My agent Jess Mileo and the team at InkWell Management. From our first conversation in 2020, Jess has been in my corner—willing to listen to every wild pitch I throw her way and pushing me to write daring, important, and joyful stories.

My editor Rachel Diebel, who read my ideas and pushed me to make them a story worth telling. This book started in a very different place; and, even though we changed a lot, Rachel always got Linus and Etta and believed they needed to be out in the world.

The team at Feiwel & Friends and Macmillan, including Jean Feiwel, Helen Seachrist, L. Whitt, Jackie Dever, Ronnie Ambrose, and Abigail L. Dela Cruz.

My family members, who always remind me to hold on to my life outside of writing as tightly as I hold on to my writing.

My friends, old and new.

My therapist.

My tattoo artists—Carrie, Jen, Emma, V., Fer, Patrick, Brooke, Kelly, and Kelly—who remind me about the power of art, healing, collaboration, and creation.

Anyone who has ever watched Winnie, allowing me to write.

I have often wondered how to best be myself in the world, and at almost forty years old, I'm still figuring it out. Thank you to everyone who has made space for others to change.

Thank you for reading this Feiwel & Friends book.
The friends who made **LINUS AND ETTA COULD USE A WIN**
possible are:

JEAN FEIWEL, PUBLISHER

LIZ SZABLA, VP, ASSOCIATE PUBLISHER

RICH DEAS, SENIOR CREATIVE DIRECTOR

ANNA ROBERTO, EXECUTIVE EDITOR

HOLLY WEST, SENIOR EDITOR

KAT BRZOZOWSKI, SENIOR EDITOR

DAWN RYAN, EXECUTIVE MANAGING EDITOR

KIM WAYMER, PRODUCTION MANAGER

EMILY SETTLE, EDITOR

RACHEL DIEBEL, EDITOR

FOYINSI ADEGBONMIRE, EDITOR

BRITTANY GROVES, ASSISTANT EDITOR

L. WHITT, DESIGNER

HELEN SEACHRIST, SENIOR PRODUCTION EDITOR

KELLY MARKUS, PRODUCTION EDITORIAL ASSISTANT

Follow us on Facebook or visit us online at mackids.com.
Our books are friends for life.